The
Legend
of
Redenta
Tiria

Salvatore Niffoi

The
Legend
of
Redenta
Tiria

TRANSLATED BY SHAUN WHITESIDE

WILLIAM HEINEMANN: LONDON

Published by William Heinemann, 2008

2 4 6 8 10 9 7 5 3 1

Copyright © Adelphi Edizioni S.P.A Milano, 2005

English translation © Shaun Whiteside, 2008

Salvatore Niffoi has asserted his right under the Copyright, Designs and Patents Act,
1988, to be identified as the author of this work

First published in Italian in 2005 under the title *La Leggenda di Redenta Tiria*
by Adelphi Edizioni, Milan, Italy

First published in Great Britain in 2008 by
William Heinemann
Random House, 20 Vauxhall Bridge Road,
London SW1V 2SA

www.rbooks.co.uk

Addresses for companies within The Random House Group Limited can be found at:
www.randomhouse.co.uk/offices.htm

The Random House Group Limited Reg. No. 954009

A CIP catalogue record for this book
is available from the British Library

ISBN: 9780434016990

The Random House Group Limited supports The Forest Stewardship
Council (FSC), the leading international forest certification organisation. All our
titles that are printed on Greenpeace approved FSC certified paper carry the FSC
logo. Our paper procurement policy can be found at: www.rbooks.co.uk/environment

Mixed Sources
Product group from well-managed
forests and other controlled sources
www.fsc.org Cert no. TT-COC-2139
© 1996 Forest Stewardship Council
FSC

Typeset by SX Composing DTP, Rayleigh, Essex
Printed and bound in Great Britain by
CPI Mackays, Chatham, ME5 8TD

Contents

Part Two Of Life Regained and Other Stories

To a frail friend carried off by the Voice

To Cristina

What the devil eats away, what he goes on eating away in people, is reasonable suffering.

João Guimarães Rosa, *Grande Sertão*

As if his ears had been unblocked, he heard, very clearly, the voice of the Mother of Men . . .

Mario Vargas Llosa, *The War at the End of the World*

Part One

The Village of the Belts

1

Abacrasta

Abaca, Abaco, Abacuc . . .You won't find Abacrasta, the name of my village, in any encyclopaedia, or on any map. No one in the outside world knows the place, because it numbers only one thousand eight hundred and twenty-seven souls, nine thousand sheep, one thousand seven hundred goats, nine hundred and thirty cows, two hundred and fifty television sets, four hundred and ninety cars and one thousand one hundred and sixty-three mobile telephones.

Abacrasta fame has spread only to the surrounding district, where it is known as 'the Village of the Belts'. In Melagravida, Ispinarva, Oropische, Piracherfa or Orotho, when someone from Abacrasta passes by, the people make the sign of the cross and wonder: 'When will it be his turn?'

No one dies of old age in Abacrasta, death never creeps up on anyone. Once they reach a certain age all the men, sensing their imminent end, undo their trousers as though they were about to do their business, slip off their belts and tie them round their necks. Women use ropes. Some use guns, slash their wrists, drown themselves, but they are few, very few, compared to those who hang themselves. In the groves of Abacrasta there is not a single tree that has not done service as a gallows.

This curse, which drives the inhabitants of Abacrasta out of their minds and convinces them that opening the door of the void is as easy as opening a bottle of cold beer, is timeless, lost somewhere in the first nightmares dreamt in ancient times, it is said, by one Eracliu Palitta, the village's founder. Eracliu was a goatherd who travelled from far across the sea in search of fresh mountain air. He stopped at the foot of a cliff that looked like the head of a big white calf and there he impregnated Artemisa Crapiolu, a blind woman who, by dint of following her goats, had developed feet as hard as stones.

They converted the sheep-pen into a house and settled down together. They had eighteen children and the handsomest of them all, Istenfalu, looked like a cross between a boar and a mule. They weaned their children on lumps of curd and rye bread, and to quench their thirst, they drew water with a cork ladle from the spring of Abacrasta, from which the village took its name. That water, even today, is thick as mastic oil and bears the acrid flavour of cuckoo-pint leaves.

Eracliu's children interbred, producing a strain of unsettled folk; their roots fixed in the past and their heads thrown forwards to sniff the future. From this commingling of blood were born catchers of bronze-beaked birds, highwaymen, cannibals, goat-breeders and horse-trainers.

In their youth these sons and daughters developed the habit of throwing their parents into the ravine where the mouflon sheep live. As soon as they had grown up they began to hang themselves from the branches of the willow trees along the banks of the River Alenu. And since then, Abacrasta has remained the same; and every year, as harvest season approaches, clouds of bronze-beaked birds arrive from far away, and scatter the fields with venomous droppings that burn three-quarters of the crops.

Today, the people of Abacrasta still live from the produce of the meagre soil: grain, milk, meat, olives, wine, grapes, cork, fruit, potatoes, calf-skin. The inhabitants of Abacrasta have their shoes and belts made to measure by two master cobblers, Alipio Cordiolu, a descendant of Nannaru, and Agustinu Candela, the son of Genuario, who hanged himself from the banisters five years ago. They make their belts very long, to go twice round the waist, and sear the owner's initials into them.

Everything else comes from outside; cars, washing machines, mobile telephones, fridges, sewing machines, computers, televisions, milking machines, fashion, ideas. Even Abacrastan shepherds come from far away, because the young men of the town no longer know how to bend their backs, and no longer want to get dung on their shoes or end up smelling of sheep.

I am Battista Graminzone, retired registrar of Abacrasta council. I have never been an ordinary unthinking administrator. Stamping documents and issuing certificates was the only way I could find to earn a living, but one thing always troubled me: why the people of my village renounced the gift of life as deliberately and easily as they did. So I began to write, first to pass the time – I have always been a bachelor – then, as I leafed through the old papers stored in the archives, out of curiosity, and finally, from the moment Redenta the blind woman arrived in Abacrasta, for pleasure.

I signed my last burial permit on the thirteenth of August six years ago, when the village's wave of suicides came to an apparently miraculous end.

One day in late summer, when the sun pierced the cork trees and the hot wind made the windows rattle, Redenta Tiria arrived in the village, a blind woman with hair that shone like a raven's wings, her feet bare.

'Where does Micheli Isoppe live?' she asked the master-blacksmith of the neighbourhood of Mumucone.

'Hundred yards to your right, then go up the hill by the church and you'll find yourself right in front of his house. He's got red geraniums on the windowsill. If he doesn't open up immediately, knock harder, because when he locks himself away in his workshop he wouldn't even hear a gun go off.'

He hadn't noticed that Redenta was blind.

'*Medas grascias!*' replied the woman, walking away in the shadow of the walls.

The master-blacksmith Antoni Sapa watched after her for a while. The pavement trembled as she went, walking on tiptoes, hoisting her skirt to her knees to air her legs. Her black hair fell to her hips like a long cloak. Redenta disappeared down the alleyway, and Antoni went back to blowing his forge. Among the sparks that the bellows threw into the chimney hood, he thought he saw the face of a Madonna.

2

Mannoi* Graminzone

My grandfather, Menelau Graminzone, died with his teeth
chattering, stretching his legs like a dog. It was Christmas
Eve, 1950. I had turned seven that November, and had
been given special permission to stay up for Midnight
Mass.

That night Mannoi Graminzone left dinner halfway
through and went back to the sheep-pen, saying that he had
to check on the animals.

'You'll catch your death! Don't even think about going
out in that weather!'

At dawn Tziu† Luisi found him hanging from the big oak
tree, the one that marks the border between the field of Sas
Animas and the Sanctuary of the Madonna of the Harvest.

* *Mannoi / Mannai* — grandfather / grandmother.
† *Tziu / Tzia* — uncle / aunt

His eyes were wide open and his ears had been nibbled by field mice. My grandmother, Mannai Juvanna, to calm me, hugged me to her and said, without crying:

'Don't worry, Battì, all the men in Abacrasta die like that!'

His was the first corpse I ever saw, hanging from the branch like a ham, curing in the air.

With his pruning knife my grandfather had removed a small bough from the tree, by moonlight, lest he be hidden among the twigs, because then the crows might have had sport with him and left nothing but his bare bones. He had chosen that particular place as carefully as a shaman marking out a circle for a ritual. A few days before, he had cut back the brambles around the trunk and carried away all the stones. Twenty yards from the oak tree, where the sun's eye began dancing at dawn, he had placed a cross: two olive branches tied with wire, and a photograph of himself as a soldier.

In the picture he was wearing a cap with a smooth leather peak, a smoke-grey jacket, and a double-sided cartridge case. God alone knows whether he ever killed anyone at the front. He used to laugh as he told me about the Great War, as if it was just a little story, telling me that he had been a pilot who signed documents with an X. I'll never forget him pretending to be an aeroplane.

'Zoooooooommm, zooom, zoooo . . . ratatatata, tatata, tata . . .'

He spread his arms like a hawk and circled the kitchen table, firing at the dresser and the mouth of the bread-oven:

'*Tatata, tata, ratatata* . . . Into the trench, Battì! Into the trench, the shrapnel's raining down!'

Laid out in his coffin he seemed older, as though he had lived twice as long as he had. His face bore a curious sneer, the expression of someone who had not loved life, who had been born out of duty and had done everything else out of duty as well: loved, had children, walked, worked.

'His time had come,' his relations said.

As she wept for him, showing a mask of deep-set wrinkles, Mannai Juvanna accepted the condolences of the peasants and replied to them all in the same way:

'The Voice called him, and he obeyed!'

Where did that voice come from, who did it belong to?, I wondered anxiously. I was a good and obedient child, so when would it call me? One day when we were on our own, picking plums in the garden, I asked my grand-mother:

'Grandma! What does that voice say when it calls people?'

She scratched the back of my neck with her hard nails and replied:

'"Ajò! Get ready, for your time has come!" That's all it

says, Battì. Then it holds out an invisible hand and takes you away.'

From that moment onwards my life was spent waiting for that voice, for that hand that would lead me away.

3

Pascale Prunizza

At secondary school I had made a friend called Pascale
Prunizza. He was a few years older than me and had been
held back a year. He didn't understand the first thing about
theorems or periodic analysis, but he could fire a catapult
like a sniper, and identify birds' eggs from a mile away. He
could identify all kinds of different birds' nests, and knew
how to train snakes and lizards. When lessons were over,
he threw his books on his chair and ran into the countryside
to help his father herd and milk the sheep. He had also
learned to make cheese, although none of us ever
discovered how. Pascale was tall as a pole, with a bump on
his nose from head-butting his primary school teacher, and
when he fought with his classmates he flared his nostrils
and emitted strange grunting sounds.

The first time he took me to the sheepfold it was the

depths of winter. It was raining, rain that felt like grated ice. The next morning we were to have a French oral test, and we could barely distinguish that language – with its *wees* and *mays* and *pookwas* – from the cries of animals. It was no use to us at all.

'When are we ever going to meet a real Frenchman in Abacrasta?' Pascale said, showing teeth already stained yellow with nicotine.

'It might be useful for when the emigrants come home on holiday,' I replied.

'What are you talking about? They can bloody well speak Sardinian like everybody else.'

To make cigarettes, Pascale picked up stubs from the street and crumbled them on to a rectangular piece of tissue paper. He rolled it all into a fat tube, lit it with wax matches and smoked it right down to the end, holding the remains between his finger and thumb.

'And when are you going to decide to grow up and smoke?' he often said to me, teasingly.

That far-off winter day, in the little sheepfold, he persuaded me to take my first drag. I felt a searing burn right down into my stomach, as though I had been forced to drink boiling pitch. To restore me, having done the damage, he scooped a bowl of sweet cheese from the curd-barrel and cut a big slice off it with his knife.

'Eat this, you dickhead, it'll put broth in your bollocks!'

Pascale's cheese tasted of fresh grass and honey. Before

we left, he separated the white mass from the whey, cut it into pieces and, pressing it with his hands, slipped the cheese into little baskets to drip its moisture away and assume its proper shape. From a niche in the dry-stone wall he took a dusty bottle and uncorked it with his teeth.

'Take a swig of this stuff, because in a moment I'm going to show you something amazing up behind Thunder Hill.'

My guts fired up once more, and my blood began to boil.

'Bloody hell, that's lethal! What is it, petrol?'

'Near enough,' he said with a laugh. 'Now let's make sure we're not late. Remember that when you get back, when the school bell rings, you go and stand in St Itria's alleyway and mingle with all the others when they come out of school, so your mother doesn't notice.'

We climbed a path half-blocked by bushes and dry-stone walls and, turning right towards Thunder Hill, we walked quite a way along the River Sappaiu. It had stopped sleeting and the sun fell on the holly leaves, making them shine like stars.

'Mind you don't faint, and hold on tight to your balls, because otherwise you'll find them in your throat!'

Both the excitement and the alcohol were beginning to take effect. I was drenched with sweat, and every now and again it felt like an animal with cold feet was walking up and down my spine.

14

'Is this surprise of yours going to be a good one, Pascà?' I asked him.

He didn't reply, but went on walking, face tilted to the sun. When we drew near to a stone wall, he dropped to his knees and beckoned me, with a series of sharp gestures, to do the same. Then he brought his hand to his mouth in the shape of a pair of scissors, and mimed the act of cutting. I immediately understood that from that moment on I was not even to breathe.

Inside a pen, four wild stallions, tethered by their hooves with iron chains, were leaning their muzzles on a little gate cobbled together out of old tables. They whinnied lazily, spewing foamy steam into the air. Their coats gleamed black, with bluish tints.

'Don't move,' he said in a low voice.

He climbed a wild pear tree to get into the pen, jumped over the wall, and slowly approached the horses. He started stroking their manes and backs and then, with a little rusty key, freed them one by one from their chains. He opened the gate, dismissing them with a slap on the back, and let them run towards the plain.

'Go on! Go on! Off you go! You were born to gallop.'

Pascale played this prank on Dineddu Podargu, the horses' owner, every now and again. He couldn't stand Podargu, because he whipped the stallions until they bled, and always kept them locked up in the pen.

'He's a bastard,' he said to me. 'Anyone who treats

15

animals like that ought to be made to eat shit and drink nothing but piss.'

We went home with our pockets full of red arbutus berries, eating handfuls at a time.

Before he said goodbye to me, he looked me in the face and asked:

'Battì! Have you ever seen such beautiful horses?'

When he spoke about horses, or recounted his grandmother's dreams, Pascale Prunizza opened his eyes wide, like chestnuts about to burst from their shells. He had lost his grandfather in the War, and since then, Mintonia Sulapis had seen nothing in her sleep but warriors doing battle with three-headed monsters, sacked cities and bloodbaths that always ended at dawn, when the nurses woke her up for her morning coffee. Then, until lunchtime, she went on hearing sabres clashing in battle, the hooves of advancing horses pounding the earth, the rattle of artillery darkening the sky with clouds of gunpowder.

'You hear them, Pascalè? They're coming! Go and hide in the barn, if they find you they'll cut off your head!'

Pascale, who feared neither the living nor the dead, drew his long-bladed knife and replied:

'Don't worry, Mannà, if they come I'll defend you.'

Once, in late spring, Mannai Mintonia told him a strange dream, one which really did frighten him and worried him for quite some time. She dreamed of a crimson bull, with long metal horns and hooves sharp as claws. It had come out of a big bronze urn, and for thirteen months it had wandered the countryside around Abacrasta, in search of Dineddu Podargu's horses. When it found them, it disembowelled them and, before disappearing, devoured their guts. It left the animals on the ground in the pen, their flesh exposed to the wasps and flies.

At the end of the dream a child, dressed in white like an altar-boy and swinging a chasuble that gave off a scent of burned incense, ran along the dry-stone wall of the pen shouting:

'Why? Why?'

From a long way off the wind carried a faint voice, as though a drunken god had been born in the oak-grove of Sas Nastulas:

'Because it's your turn next.'

The face of that child, in Mannai Mintonia's dream, bore the features of Pascale.

'Beware the red bull, Pascalè! It's still abroad in these parts, looking for souls to carry off!'

Pascale's grandmother wasn't mad or overtired, it was just that she saw in her dreams what others couldn't see in reality, she sensed the direction of destiny. One evening she advised one of her son Paulu's friends not to take the tractor to go milking:

'Gonà,' she said, 'I dreamt last night that you were

flying like an angel, and your wings were drenched in blood. Perhaps you should leave the tractor at home for a few days, and walk to the sheepfold.'

Gonario Ruzzanca had jokingly replied:

'And you expect me to come back on foot as well? Cars weren't invented to be left outside the house, Tzia Mintò!'

The next day, Gonario set off to see to his sheep with two sacks of fodder in the boot, but didn't get so far as a mile from home. Just beyond the hill of Loroddai, at the third bend the tractor jumped the gutter and ended up going over the Sos Astores precipice. They spent seven days looking for him. But all they recovered was a photograph of him taken at the carnival, dressed as a black angel.

All that summer Pascale saw nothing but red bulls and horse carcasses wherever he looked. In the water, in the air, in the road. Everywhere he went, he looked around suspiciously, brought a cupped hand to his ear and said:

'Hear that? You hear that sound of hooves? It's the red bull coming to take me away.'

One morning I set off early to see him, because we had arranged to meet at the Mascrubò fold, for the shearing party. His mother told me he had gone out before dawn:

'He didn't even drink his coffee. He just put his bag over his shoulder and ran off like a fury.'

Pascale wasn't at the Mascrubò fold. The Voice had

called him elsewhere. I found him before midday, hanging from the wild pear tree that guarded the pen with its bitter fruit, the tree he had used to climb in. In the middle of the clearing, lying side by side like weary children, lay the stallions shot by Dineddu Podargu during the night.

4

Bernardu Solitariu

In Abacrasta they called him Bernardu Solitariu, because there were no other births on the island the day he came into the world. It was the fourth of August, and the sun devoured the shadows in the street in its golden jaws.

'When will this sweltering heat come to an end? If it goes on like this we're all going to die!' said Liciniu Poddicale, sipping at a glass of beer that was as hot as a bowl of broth.

'Some die, others are born!' added Arturo, the barman, turning to the company of idlers. 'You know Tuniedda Curre-Curre gave birth this morning?'

'That whore?' asked Coseme Zicoria. 'She'll have her work cut out choosing a surname for it, out of a hundred possible fathers! Bit of a lottery, that!'

*

When word reached Abacrasta that Bernardu was the only child born that Friday in the whole of Sardinia, there was a small celebration and, inspired by wine, a group of drunks christened him Bernardu Su Solitariu, 'the Lonely One'. In the register of births, marriages and deaths, Bernardu's father is still listed as 'unknown', and he bears the surname of his mother, Tuniedda Peleas, known as Curre-Curre, or 'the Fast One', because of her profession.

Running through the alleyways of the neighbourhood of Gattulinos, Bernardu lengthened only his legs, while his trunk stayed short and fat, like a barrel. His arms weren't long enough to reach his flies, and every time he wanted to piss he had to genuflect like a dog, dropping to his right knee. The little folds on his eyebrows and his spoon-shaped nose made him look like some ancient animal that had crawled out of a hole in the ground.

From earliest childhood, he had lived up to the nickname that the boozers had given him: he always played on his own, and wouldn't let anyone near him. Those who tried to tame him and make him less bad-tempered still bear the marks: teeth-marks, scars inflicted with iron or stone.

Because of his violent disposition, many people thought he was the natural son of Adamu Cerdone, a stranger to the village who had taken to banditry and kidnapping. Bernardu's mother Tuniedda Peleas had been seen with him many times walking to and from the Carvonaios cave, where Adamu had one of his lairs.

Bernardu was rustic in his manners, and no one could stand up to him, not even his mother. One day when she denied him permission to go to the harvest festival, he jumped on her and tried to strangle her. Had Dariu Carburo not arrived just in time, he would have finished her off and thrown her in the well.

'Are you mad, laying your hands on your mother?'

'I have neither mother nor father, I'm nobody's son!' replied Solitariu, spitting with rage.

He was thirteen at the time, and went to the harvest festival regardless. Climbing to the top of the mountain of Nidu Abilas, he looked down at the peasants. Singing a hymn to the Madonna of the Harvest, they were working away with their scythes and stripping the fields like a flock of locusts. The women wore hobnailed boots and tied the sheaves together to form a bale which they then carried on their backs. The younger ones assembled the sheaves in a clearing and turned the spit roasts in the shade of a lean-to set up against the side of the sanctuary.

When the lard dripped sizzling onto the flames, and the skin of the suckling pigs turned to crackling, the wind wafted up a cloud of aromas that made his mouth water.

'Go on then,' he said to himself. 'The best is yet to come!'

That lunch was the kind that's never forgotten: round,

hand-pulled macaroni with mutton sauce, roasted meat, mutton stew, blue cheese, raw onions, fresh tomatoes and rivers of dark red wine. In the evening, before the townsfolk went home, they danced around the fires, and had the crop blessed by the priest, Don Attilio.

Solitariu waited for the moon to rise and light his way and, leaping from rock to rock, he reached a spot behind the sanctuary. The fires were still smouldering, because by tradition they were left to go out in the dead of night. He picked up two glowing brands and flung them on to the stack of freshly mown sheaves. As the first tongues of flame rose flickering into the sky, Solitariu threw himself on the ground and started rolling in the straw with joy.

At the age of twenty, when his mother died, Bernardu Solitariu found himself at a loss, with few reasons to live and many to die. He woke each morning wondering why he had ever been brought into the world, since being among other human beings brought him out in a rash.

The dermatologists in the Noroddile hospital, while keeping him at a respectable distance, diagnosed and certified his illness, which had until that moment been unknown. They discovered that as soon as anyone approached him, even with the best intentions, he began to feel an itch all over his skin, as if he was walking on a swarm of man-eating ants. After a few minutes, his body

23

was covered with boils that stung and burst, like *pane carasau** fresh from the oven.

For a few years, as he waited for the Voice to call him, he gave himself up entirely to drinking and stealing anything that came his way. It was said that one day he even killed a man for the new velvet suit he had just had made for his wedding. He also made off with the man's patent leather shoes, his cufflinks and his gold bracelet.

Thus attired, one evening he approached a singer who had come to a *festa* with her guitarist. She was a woman from Traspacadule, middle-aged and wearing a party frock, all lace and jewels. She had a voice that stole your heart, and a bosom that made your eyes pop from their sockets.

He approached her as she came into the venue near the old barracks, to put on a bit of make-up before the concert. No one ever found out what it was that Solitariu said to her. What is true is that from that night onwards, Signora Moira di Traspacadule slept in his bed and sang only for him. His rash vanished as if by magic, and the beautiful stranger, who had a little bag of magic herbs, helped him discover the will to live.

With her savings, they set up a bakery and opened a pastry shop. Moira and Solitariu's *formaggelle*, the *amaretti*, the *aranzada*, the *pan di sapa*, the *bianchini* are still remembered by everyone in Abacrasta and the surrounding

*See Glossary, page 192.

24

district. They were special, leaving a taste of vanilla honey in the mouth for ages afterwards, they were intoxicating in a way that made life more endurable – but they didn't knock your legs out from under you like strong red wine.

The secret of the Pasticceria Solimò, as the shop was called, lay in the pinch of magic herbs that Moira added to the mixtures. Their pastries were so popular that there were barely enough hours in the day to chop the almonds, beat the eggs, candy the oranges, draw out the sheets of pastry. So to keep up with all the orders they received for baptisms, christenings, weddings and communions, they took on two additional workers, Uselia and Curicia.

Never had life been so beautiful for Bernardu Solitariu, never had fate treated him so tenderly. He went to sleep laughing between Moira's breasts, and woke up smiling in her arms.

Things went on like that for almost ten years, give or take a few days. One evening when Moira told him that the magic herbs were about to run out, Solitariu felt a strange sadness fall upon him, and woke that night to find that his itch had returned. The rash was devouring him. He scratched himself until he bled, and did so till dawn, when he heard the Voice calling him:

'Ajò! Get ready, for your time has come!'

That was all it said. He slipped on his trousers and went out into the courtyard saying he was going for a walk.

'I'll be back soon,' he told his companion. 'Get the filling ready for the *pistiddus*, and prepare to glaze the *papassinus*!'

He didn't walk a hundred yards from the stone front doorstep. Closing the cellar door behind him, he hanged himself with his belt from an iron ring fixed in the ceiling. By now I had been employed by the council for three years and once all the requisite tests had been carried out it was the twenty-eighth burial certificate I signed. Only three of the deceased had died a natural death, 'of unknown illness and unknown causes', as the health officer, Dr Lampazio, ascertained. All the others had taken their lives with a knot at their throats, although this, on paper, became a bureaucratic line: 'Died in Abacrasta, district of x, day y, time approximately z, (presumed) suicide by hanging'.

5

Beneitta Trunzone

They started dressing Beneitta Trunzone as a nun from the age of three. For centuries the Trunzone family had always given one of their daughters to God, shutting her away in the closed convent of the Poor Clares of Piscopio to serve her novitiate. Then, after they had taken their vows, they were usually sent to some secluded convent on the Italian mainland. Beneitta didn't know it, but even before her birth she had been destined for the life of a nun. When she fell pregnant for the sixth time, Mama Giacumina had clearly said as much to her husband Rimundu Trunzone:

'Rimù, if it's a girl, we'll offer the fruit of my womb to God!'

Rimundu pulled a face and said yes, because his wife wore the trousers in his household and, besides, a daughter in the countryside was worse than useless. A Trunzone

27

without a nun for a daughter was going against tradition, it would mean losing family properties and the friendship of relatives. Had he and his wife suffered the disgrace of bringing only boy-children into the world, they would have had to make up for it by giving a field to the bishop or signing over twenty head of cattle to the parish priest. Things had been this way since a miracle befell Anchisu Trunzone, an ancestor of the family who had escaped the wrath of God and the men of Don Carmine Ispunzale.

One night, for a bet, Anchisu, who was as handsome as a Nuragic bronze, and could catch women as easily as other men catch horseflies, slipped into Don Carmine's bed and took his wife, Dona Amalia di Soricò.

'Bet you aren't brave enough to fuck Don Carmine's wife!' two of his drinking partners said to him one evening.

He smiled and curled the tips of his blond moustache, before whispering:

'What's the stake?'

'We'll bet our livestock. What about you? You haven't even got enough water to fill your jug.'

'I'll bet the most precious thing I have: my skin!'

'No point betting that, because if Don Carmine catches wind of it, you're a dead man anyway. You know he only has to think about it to have you blasted to bits!'

Fired up by the challenge and the wine in his veins, Anchisu drew from his pocket a gold watch, the kind with a cover and a little chain:

'Is this enough for you? Bastards!'

In order to fulfil the bet, the ancestor of the Trunzones asked for a month's grace and a white mare on which, starting the following day, he began to prance back and forth below Dona Amalia's windows. He slicked his hair with mastic oil and combed it back, in line with the prevailing fashion, drew his sideburns down so that they framed his chin, polished his teeth with sage leaves and dripped sea-water into his eyes to make them sparkle. He was irresistible, and his solitary parade soon attracted Dona Amalia's attention.

Don Carmine Ispunzale's wife was childless. She spent her time getting bored at the piano, and embroidering little birds on pillowcases and sheets. Don Carmine was so possessive of her that he wouldn't even let her out of the house to go to church on days of obligation.

One afternoon, when her husband had gone to the live-stock market in Bàrdulos, she tied her hair at the nape of her neck and went down to the street, on the pretext of trimming the geraniums that cascaded from the first-floor windows. Anchisu climbed down from his horse and tethered it to the iron ring hanging from the wall of the façade.

They didn't say a word to each other. Their eyes met

first, then the perfumes of their bodies: the scents of jasmine, freshly tanned leather and mandarin leaves. They threw themselves drunkenly into Don Carmine's four-poster bed, and afterwards rose exhausted from their hastily consummated bliss. Before, during and after, not so much as a syllable, nothing but moans and whimpers. They left as they had met, gazing into each other's eyes, exchanging only the scents of sheets and sight of discarded clothing.

The wild fruit of their love, stolen from Don Carmine, swelled like leavened dough in Dona Amalia's womb. In the fourth month, when the damage could no longer be concealed, Don Carmine kicked the child from his wife's belly.

'Who's the blackguard, eh? Tell me who it is, so that I may slaughter him and hang him from the bell tower of the big church! Everyone must see what happens to those who dishonour Carmine Ispunzale!'

Dona Amalia died soon after from the beating, but she never revealed Anchisu's name. It was Tzia Giuditta Sacchetta who betrayed him, in return for two dairy goats and a quail. On her way to early Mass she had seen the tethered mare, and Anchisu dancing his way out of the front door.

Don Carmine paid two hired killers to cut his head off with an axe, and his cock with a knife:

'Stuff that bastard's two heads in a bag and bring them

to me by tomorrow morning!'

Abante and Corittu went to find Anchisu in his house by
the river. When they knocked, the door fell open by itself.
There was no one inside, but a lamp burned in a corner,
the bed was still made, there was a chamber pot, and some
old shoes. They heard a voice calling them, but didn't even
have time to turn round, before they were hurled against
the wall by a shower of lead. Anchisu dragged them by the
feet and toppled them into the pool below Paparedda Falls.

As the shots rang out Don Carmine felt a sharp pain in
his chest:

'Oh *dimoniu*! That pennyroyal *sanguinaccio* I had for
dinner is giving me indigestion!'

Stumbling towards the granite sink, he fell and struck
his head against its edge. His hand stiff with agony, he
managed to turn on the tap. All that night, the drain to the
street ran with blood and water.

From that point onwards, Anchisu saw sense and raised
a family. He fathered nine daughters with Afidina Errules,
and to give thanks to God for his escape from certain
death, he had the first one shut up in the convent of the
Poor Clares of Piscopio.

They never told Beneitta Trunzone that story. She grew up
lovely as a rose, and liked to spend all day in the sun, like
a lizard. Had it been up to her, she would have spent her
life playing with dolls, watching the trucks that passed in

the street, listening to music at full volume on the radio and dancing with the other children of the neighbourhood.

She really didn't like her nun's habit, which made her look like a horned swallow. As she grew, they made a new one for her every two years, and then, when her twentieth birthday arrived, they celebrated it like a wedding. And told her to prepare herself.

'The time has come to give yourself to God, Beneì!'

She would rather have given herself to Bustianu Chitarra, who knew how to jive and who dressed like the Beatles, in gleaming goatskin boots and Nehru jackets. She knew all the words to *Yesterday*, and hated the songs of the choir as much as she hated her heavy and painful periods. But there was nothing to be done, that was how it had been, how it was, and how it would be for all eternity. On the day fixed for her departure, Beneitta heard the Voice:

'Ajò! Get ready, for your time has come!'

She put on her nun's habit, locked herself in her room and turned the record player up as loud as it would go. *Dum, da-dee-da-da-dum, da-dum, da-da-da*. She put on *Day Tripper* and bought her final one-way ticket, on a rope hooked to the wardrobe door. *Dum, da-dee-da-da-dum, da-dum, da-da-da*. Beneitta Trunzone chose to die with that music in her ears rather than wait for death in a cloister. It was July, and the year was 1968. Students and workers were protesting on television. In Abacrasta, where time's heart was made of stone, I recorded the year's fifth suicide.

32

6

Genuario Candela

The cobbler Genuario Candela had been left a widower at the age of ninety-nine. He was a few months shy of his hundredth birthday, and to honour him, despite his freshly donned mourning clothes, his children, grandchildren, great-grandchildren and relatives by marriage hurled themselves into the preparations for the great festivity.

His wife Luisedda Corrasi had been carried off by some obscure illness that had consumed her flesh and her bones. On the day of the funeral, when Gigi Trumbone was called to put the lid on the coffin, she was reduced to nothing, and would have fitted into a bucket. Only her face had remained intact, her lips corrugated with pain, her mouth toothless, her ash-coloured hair and her deep-sea-blue eyes that no one had managed to close. The rest of her body looked as if it had been pecked by chickens.

Genuario wept for her like a child, and from that day onwards he was unable to smile. Before then, just looking at him would have put you in a good mood, his belly stretched out in his velvet waistcoat and a ready laugh for every occasion. Tziu Genuario could draw water from a stone, he could see the funny side even in life's tragedies. When Valeriu Cambuzu hanged himself with a belt made by Tziu Genuario, the cobbler declared:

'I should have left him in his underwear! Belts are for people who know how to wear trousers!'

The morning they found Taniella Calasciu burnt in her bed Genuario was measuring two customers for shoes. They insisted that the fire had been started by a candle that she kept lit on the bedside table, and he had a quick retort, as always:

'Nonsense – it was a spark from between her legs! Don't you remember how red she always was, as if she had St Anthony's fire in her cheeks?'

The younger inhabitants of the village went to his workshop to hear tales of damned souls and filthy jokes, of which he had an endless repertoire. In full flight, he would finish one and begin another, without interruption. I always suspected that he made them up on the spot, because they were never the same, and the places, situations and characters were constantly changing.

He wasn't a bad soul, Tziu Genuario. His habit of teasing his fellows had been with him since he had burnt his

34

tongue with caustic soda. It was August, and he was dying of heat, every pore of his skin was exploding. Eyes blurred with sweat, he opened the cupboard where he hid his little bottle of brandy to quench his thirst and, by mistake, he picked up the bottle of soda solution that he used to clean the pitch off his tools. He cursed all the saints and Madonnas and, from that day forth, in Abacrasta, he was called Brujore – the Burning One.

His workshop, on the top floor of his house, faced the church of Santu Predu, and there were times when more people went to have their shoes made by Genuario than went to the parish priest for confession. The finest calf's leather, first-rate craftsmanship guaranteed. Despite the competition from Alipio Cordiolu and his son, customers came to Genuario from all over the province and the rest of the island. Wherever there was sheep dung, there you would find his boots, wherever there were clothes of fustian or velvet, there you would also find his decorated belts, with the bronze buckle and the owner's initials.

More recently, with the rise in ethnic identity, the fashion for velvet suits and sheperds leather shoes called *cosinzos* had spread throughout the island, even reaching the seaside towns. Suddenly Abacrasta was attracting swarms of politicians and journalists, singers and foot-ballers, people with white feet, mincing dandies whose like the villagers had only ever seen on postcards or on television. Genuario had looked one city-dweller in the eye and said:

'But what do you want with shoes like these? You live by the sea, you don't have to graze sheep. You should be walking around barefoot or in sandals!'

The work mounted up, but Genuario wouldn't hear of enlarging the workshop.

'It'll stay just as I've known it!' he said to his sons. 'And even when I go, I don't want so much as a nail to be added to it. No machinery, and no ready-made uppers! Go on using your hands, they're the things that'll put bread on your table!'

In Abacrasta Genuario's shop was more popular than the library, it was the true cultural centre of the village, where people discussed stolen animals, horrible deaths and lean years. Until Luisedda's death, Genuario was forever tidying up, working at his last like a young man. After she died he didn't touch a thing. He climbed the steps from his house to the workshop, up the spiral staircase made for him by Pinzitta, a master ironworker. He looked at the tools, like dead things now. The rolls of wire, the awls, the wooden forms, the scrapers, the hammers, the pincers no longer spoke to him, they had been left voiceless. There was no point living like this.

In the morning, when his sons went to wake him for the big celebration of his hundredth birthday they found the bed unmade and a note written in pencil.

'*Adiosu*! I'm off to join your mother.'

He hadn't asked forgiveness, he hadn't written anything else, just those few words, before following the invisible hand of the Voice. At dawn, when the smell of calf's leather and rubber still lingered between the walls, he had cut a long strip of leather and knotted it to the handrail of the banisters. Then, calling to his wife in a low voice, he had dropped like a dead weight in the stairwell.

'Luisè! Luisè! Make yourself beautiful, I'm on my way!'

7

The cork tree of the Cambaleddos

The Cambaleddos, eight brothers and sisters, got their nickname from the *gambali*, or leggings, that they had worn as children. Both their father Boelle and mother Cadirina were killed in a car accident, ending up under an articulated lorry while driving their three-wheeled van to their vegetable plot. The children just about managed to identify them by the fact that their mother was wearing a ring with an acorn-shaped coat of arms, and their father had gold incisors.

Boelle Camandula, back in the days when he lived and laughed, looked like a wild cat, ready to tear someone to pieces. Yet in reality he was as sweet as pie, and let his little grandchildren wrestle him to the ground as if he was a bag of potatoes. He had spent his life as a miner in Oropische, and returned to Abacrasta as an old man, to work the vegetable plot at Cumideri and make cork hives for bee-keepers. In the summer he watered the plot twice, early in the morning and then again in the evening. He spent the day amongst the furrows, treating, planting, binding and picking. During the hot hours of the afternoon he sat down on a stone bench behind the shed wall, carving pieces of wood with a file and a knife.

He set off while the sun still slept, after throwing into his knapsack some bits of bread, a bit of cheese, a slice of pancetta and a jerrycan of wine. He loaded his wife Cadirina on to the back and off they went, the three-wheeler backfiring away, mingling the smell of petrol with the odour of goat droppings. Phut, phut, phut, phut, phut, it seemed to fart as it climbed the hill of Sos Lacheddos.

In the winter he dug the soil and spread seasoned manure; he sheltered the earth from the sun and the cold wind with reed mats; he planted carrots, cardoons, leeks, radishes, fennel and chicory; he pruned the vines in the bower and the orange trees, trimming the foliage, removing unwanted shoots and suckers with his fingertips.

Boelle and Cadirina were so happy it was as if they hadn't been born in Abacrasta. Fate had been kind to them, even lavish. Eight children, four boys and four girls, all so healthy and beautiful they could have won prizes. They had all married well, and had jobs in offices and hospitals and in the factories on the Ordolai plain. The idea of emigrating, of seeking work elsewhere, as so

39

many did, hadn't even occurred to them. Work had sought them out, life had kissed them on the forehead, creating, inevitably, a certain amount of envy and discontent in Abacrasta.

'Incredible good luck Camandula's kids all have, there's not one of them out of work! God knows how they managed to have such good fortune! Contacts, it must be! All contacts!'

Boelle, a practising Christian, thanked God Almighty each morning for having been so generous to his family. At table, before his morning coffee, he never failed to voice a thought for the Lord. On the day on which he didn't live to see the night, he had sat down, hands folded, opposite his wife, and prayed:

'Guide us once more today, oh Lord, towards the straight, sure way that leads to Your eternal kingdom! Your life is our road: by the light of Your holy suffering we make our way towards You, for You are our crown.'

Boelle Camandula was known to understand the voices of the stars. That dawn, when the stars still shone like glow-worms in the sky, he tried to listen to them, but they didn't tell him anything precise. Instead he heard a different voice that came from farther away and spoke an unfamiliar tongue:

'Alè! Alè! Ajò!' it exclaimed from time to time.

Later, what they picked up from the road looked like dirty rags. Patches of gleaming oil and blood on the tarmac. Bits of shoe, the visor of a beret, sheet metal, a hand, a little image of the Corpus Domini.

A month after the funerals, the Cambaleddos all met up in the shed at the Cumideri vegetable plot. They had fixed the date as the thirtieth day, a full month after the church memorial service. It was an evening in May. In Frate Indovino's almanac the stars showed joy and good fortune. The siblings stayed shut inside until the moon appeared over the hill like an enormous slipper. No one knows what passed between them during those long hours, because there was not another living soul around, and nothing in the sky but eight barn owls. Their nocturnal cries were frightening, they scraped along your skin like a razor blade.

The Cambaleddos, walking in a line like altar boys, made for the Plateau of Asphodels, where the souls of suicides are said to fly transformed into bats. At the centre of the plateau stood an enormous cork oak tree with eight branches. To the sound of music, the flowery tips of the asphodels began to dance and, one at a time, Cambaleddos helped each other to climb into the oak tree.

The story is still told in Abacrasta of how the youngest one, Ettorinu, before throwing himself off with the rope around his neck, had a moment's hesitation and asked the others:

'Why are we doing this?'

'So that we may be born again! How stupid are you?' replied Dittinna, the oldest sister.

They were found by Bitheddu the goatherd, hanging from the twisted ropes, turning in the air to the tune of a carillon. When the Attorney General himself informed me of this, I couldn't believe my ears, and thought it was a bad joke. Just to make sure, before the rumour went speeding round the village, I walked to the Plateau of the Asphodels. The police had laid them out on the ground and covered them with white sheets. From a distance they looked like big blocks of talc.

8

Bantine Pica, the Mayor

'With reference to Art. 144 of the State Ordinance, Royal Decree 9/7/1939 no. 1238, it is recorded that on this day 3 July 1978, in the place of Piazza Su Cumbentu, on the central balcony of Abacrasta Town Hall, the body was found of a person identified as Bantine Pica, son of Giasone, born in . . . His burial is authorised in accordance with Article 16 of Permanent Council Regulations.'

Bantine Pica was born in Abacrasta on a day when water and mud fell from the sky. His mother, gritting her teeth, drenched the pillow with her bitter sweat and his father ended up all alone in the kitchen, frantically shuffling a pack of cards. When the child who would be the King of Coins appeared, the midwife came in, screeching like a jaybird stuck in mistletoe:

'A boy, Giasò! A boy! As soon as I've finished washing him, come and see him! He's a gem! A jewel!'

The bell tower clock struck five. Giasone stubbed out his cigarette in his half-empty glass and, slowly, got up to walk over to the window. His muscles were relaxed and his mouth felt burnt, as if he had eaten hot ashes.

The rain painted muddy birds on the window, which opened their wings for a second before flowing together into a dirty splodge on the windowsill. For three days, it had been like this. No one had ever seen such a horrible July. For three days and three nights the sky had done nothing but spew forth blood, and Telesia hadn't been able to give birth. A terrible year, 1935.

Giasone's full bladder forced him to cross his legs. Suddenly, unable to hold on any longer, he opened the door and went and pissed under the awning. Then, counting his footsteps, he came back to the bedroom. Forty-three steps.

'This child's going to live for forty-three years!' he thought to himself. 'And not a day more!'

Giasone Pica was a shepherd who, like many of the inhabitants of Abacrasta, believed in fate and pre-destination. One day when Alipinta the witch told him that a lightning flash would kill twelve sheep, he sent her off with a flea in her ear. After the storm he went to the sheepfold and found twelve sheep dead, burnt and with their bellies in the air.

Another time she told him to be careful, and to prepare for a bad year, because his cheese would be devoured by worms. A month later, in the cellar all he found was three inches of worms, a finger thick. From that moment onwards he too began to read the premonitory signs of fate.

He had married in February, in the rain, in his black suit, with three stones in one pocket and a sprig of butcher's broom and one of arbutus, or strawberry tree, in the other. Before he went to collect his bride, he looked at himself in the mirror and sang a rhyme nine times:

> Butcher's broom
> Fills me with rheum
> Strawberry tree
> Puts pounds on me.[*]

Now Giasone took his son in his arms and kissed him on the forehead.

'You're as lovely as the King of Coins!'

The child opened his eyes wide as if he had understood, then began to whimper, his moans following the rhythm of the rain.

[*]Sa mela'e vrusciu
m'achet su tusciu
sa mela 'e lidone
lardu mi ponete.

'If you don't object, we'll call him Constantine, like the Roman emperor.'

'Your will is what counts in this house, Giasò. But perhaps it would be better to call him Bantine, in the Sardinian manner. What do you say?'

'I say it's fine,' he replied.

Giasone returned to the kitchen, drained the last drops of wine from the bottle and, tightly clutching his playing cards, went out into the rain in search of company for the first game of the day.

Thus it was that Bantine Pica came into the world, amongst wine, tobacco, cards, sweat, mud and Roman emperors.

Bantine grew up strong in arm and brain. By the age of eleven he had shoulders like a chest of drawers and muscles hard as the knots in a holm oak. He wore glasses because of his imperfect eyesight, which forced him to scrutinise his fellow men and surrounding objects with apparent amazement. He was so intelligent that his parents were obliged to send him to university.

Even as a little boy he amused himself with tins, bits of wire and the like, building cable cars and watermills. He was precise in everything that he did: eating, dressing, walking, studying, playing cards. He never missed a point when playing *briscola*, *scopone* or *tressette*. He memorised all the cards played by his adversaries and studied their moves, and when his turn came they hadn't a prayer.

He had inherited the vice of card-playing from his father, who had put them in his hands when he was still in his baby-walker. It was through cards that Giasone taught him numbers, colours and his first words. He hid the pack behind his back and then, one by one, held the cards up in front of the boy's nose and set them out on the tray of the baby-walker.

'What is this one, my son?'

'The ace, Papa!' he crowed.

'And this one?'

Bantine slowly moved his finger over the card, as though it were a magic wand. 'Four!'

'And this other one?'

Bantine smiled, his eyes rolling wildly as though they didn't belong to him:

'The king, Papa!'

Each time he guessed that card, Giasone stroked the back of his neck.

'Well done, my child! Always remember that this is the KING of coins, your KING!'

Bantine pushed his toes against the baby-walker and made it spin like a top.

At primary school no one came close to him in maths, science and geography, not even the teacher. Mastra Ciccina told the headmaster and the boy's parents that

Bantine was 'super-gifted', a child predisposed to calculation, reasoning and logic. Perhaps in part for that reason, the other children couldn't stand him. Mastra Ciccina worshipped him alone, and the others, the Pulicos, the Corvittu's, the Candelas, the Graminzones, didn't exist for her.

Michelittu Tapiceddu, who was better endowed in the trouser than in the brains department, told her straight to her face during a geometry lesson:

'Miss, if Bantine was big, you'd have shagged him!'

For this joke he was suspended for life from all the schools in Italy.

At the age of seventeen, Bantine designed and built a group of mechanical scarecrows to chase the birds from the fields and the vines. He used a battery, reeds stuffed with gunpowder, electric wires, ball bearings and parts salvaged from an old motorbike. The mayor alerted the authorities, and Bantine was awarded a study grant. With that he enrolled at the University of Calaris, and came out an engineer.

In those days an engineer was like a general, it wasn't like it is now, when you find unemployed engineers on every street corner. In due course, Bantine also set his sights on the office of mayor. At this time Abacrasta was linked to the other villages only by two strips of white road and a mail-coach. Bantine suggested a pilaster bridge and tarmac, and with this idea he made himself the mayor and a wealthy man. You could get from Abacrasta to Noroddile in a quarter of an hour, quite incredible.

But the hereditary illness lay in wait, like a sly dog that bites before it barks. The more Bantine earned the more he spent, especially on card games. The vice of poker ran in his blood like leukaemia. His political opponents in the Progressive Party sarcastically called him the King of Coins, because of the number of contracts that reached his office via some unknown surveyor. He didn't so much as look at women, he dreamed only of pairs and flushes, flops and four of a kind.

For some time now, though, fortune had turned her back on him. He started losing, first small sums, then big ones. One night, in the old council chamber where he met up with other players, he wagered and lost his house and his office. He was even on the point of gambling away his degree.

'I'll see you and raise you this!' he said to his associates over a big pot. He furiously threw the rolled parchment on to the table.

'With this, Mr Mayor, you can wipe your arse!' replied Umbertino Bagolaj, taking his cigarette out of his mouth. Bagolaj was a bricklayer turned entrepreneur, with forty employees. Seated around the table were Bachis Gaghisi the doctor, the lawyer Bumba and Umbertino Bagolaj. These three were all in the same clique and the same party, companions in revelry and associates in business.

'If you want your house and your honour back, then bring the land I bought at Sas Mandras into the new regulatory plans!'

The lands at Sas Mandras were set aside as pasture, two hundred hectares on the border with Noroddile, towards the town centre.

'Think what kind of residential quarter might come out of it! Villas and gardens for civil servants, professional people, businessmen: a paradise just a stone's throw from the town!'

Bantine's face darkened and for a moment he couldn't see a thing, as if the light had fled.

'But you know what they'll say in Abacrasta when they know I've gambled it all away at poker? The mask of the King of Coins has slipped at last! That's what they'll say. Our mayor has revealed himself in his true colours, a gamester, a wastrel, a greedy scoundrel who would bet his own mother just to save his skin!'

'Consider our offer, Bantine! Think about it for the rest of the night, given that it'll be dawn in two hours. If you agree, call at my office in the afternoon, I've got meetings in the morning,' added *avvocato* Bumba.

'You can't fall flat on your arse, lose everything at cards, and still be mayor!' concluded Dr Gaghisi.

Bantine looked around him, and felt a sudden burst of dignity. He brought down his hand and swept away the cards, the chips, the ashtray, the empty glasses.

'Everybody out of here! Out, I said! Get out of my sight!'

Bantine Pica was left on his own, and then the light really did go out. He closed his eyelids and tried to think of something good. He heard the music of a barrel organ, and the clattering approach of iron-shod hooves. Riorroi riorroi, riorroi riorroi. In a moment he was surrounded by a crowd of masked people dressed up as playing-card figures. The only one unmasked was the organ player, who had shoulders the size of a wardrobe and squinty eyes inflamed by tears and brandy. *Riorroi riorroi, riorroi riorroi.* He played and he danced, lifting one leg like a pissing dog. *Riorroi riorroi, riorroi riorroi.* He set his foot on a chair and then, without interrupting the music, hoisted himself on to the table. *Riorroi riorroi, riorroi riorroi.* He spat something on the ground, cleaned his lips with his tongue and asked:

'Which of you is Bantine Pica, the King of Coins?'

Bantine was puzzled for a moment, and then, seeing that he was in a dream, he replied:

'I am!'

To convince the musician of his identity he also showed his driving licence.

'You see?'

The musician's eyes chilled and turned completely white, like marbles of hardened snow. He had bitten his upper lip and a thread of blood dribbled on to his chin. He licked it and spat on the ground again.

'Ajò! Get ready, for your time has come!' he said, turning to Bantine.

The echo of that voice followed Bantine to his office on the top floor. There he shut the door and looked for the rope in his desk drawer. He put one chair on top of another until his hands reached the hook for the globe lamp. He got the noose ready and kicked himself away. A chunk of cement and mortar came away, and Bantine fell on the floor along with the lamp.

He dusted down his jacket and picked up the rope. Opening the French windows, he went out onto the balcony. The air was damp and fresh, during the night a soft dew had fallen, like a coating of iron filings. Dawn was about to break, as clear as the face of a newly washed child. It was the day of St Thomas the Apostle.

From behind the hill of Istellazzos the glare of the sun was beginning to flood the fields, the vines, the olive groves. In the square below an old woman dressed in black was waiting for the first bus, as Bantine tied the rope to the pole from which the flag fluttered on the balcony, and jumped. The town clock struck five and the streets of Abacrasta began to fill with voices.

'Help! Help!' cried the old woman, circling the square like a lunatic.

'Another misfortune?' people asked, jumping from their beds.

'Who is it this time?'
'Which part of the village?'
'Which family?'
'The mayor?'
'Oh my God, oh my God!'

9

Boranzela Coro 'e Cane

Boranzela Coro 'e Cane – Boranzela Dogheart – was so-called in Abacrasta because she wouldn't have given a drop of water to a dying man. She had inherited a fortune in farmland and buildings, but never married. Never in her life had she ever shared anything with anyone, neither her bed nor her belongings. As a child she played on her own, with talking and singing dolls, painted iron prams, realistic dolls' houses. She had a room full of toys, but she wouldn't have lent any of them to anybody, not even if they'd pinched her.

'Toys cost money!' her mother Zacinta used to say. 'Keep them for your children, you never know how fast the time goes!'

Time took its toll on her father Tilone Arvada and her mother Zacinta Bundale, and little Boranzela was left an orphan at the age of six. One evening when she had gone to sleep at Aunt Lavretha's house to keep her company, her parents forgot to switch off the gas in the kitchen, and half the neighbourhood of Ispinasanta was blown to smithereens. All that remained of the house was bare stones and rubble. From that day on, Boranzela's surviving relations adopted her as a daughter, helping her to grow up both stupid and ignorant.

The death of her parents left her entirely indifferent, Boranzela was already quite crazed and disagreeable enough on her own account. She had never had to lift a finger to get what she wanted. She asked for it and that was that. I want this, I want that and I want the other. She ordered everyone around, with the excuse that she was an only child and she had a host of aunts and uncles, all unmarried by choice. If they ever said no, as they sometimes did, she took a razor from her skirt and started issuing threats:

'I'm going to kill myself! And I'm not joking!'

Her relatives were terrified. They bought her everything she wanted, even useless things. By the age of fifteen she already had a trousseau to make a princess green with envy. Sheets, towels, clothes, cutlery. Services of fine china plates, crystal glasses, shoes, shawls which were hand-embroidered with threads of gold and silver. Twelve of everything, plus the jewels and the chestnut furniture, ordered from Tonino the carpenter and paid for in advance. For the house, she only had to choose between the ones in the neighbourhoods of Melas Ruias, Sos Poetas, Limbichìchinos, Sas Damas, Animeddas, Sos Molentes.

Boranzela's relatives bought her everything, apart from books and magazines, for these brought madness and set the brain to thinking. The Arvadas had always made their money by the sweat of their brow, by swinging billhooks, and if that wasn't enough they sometimes resorted to gunfire, because that was what made people see reason, unlike books and words. All the land that had come into their possession, beginning with the poor farmland of Muscatellones, they had expropriated with menaces and blackmail.

They had garrotted Talibiu Cheronza's cows and slashed the throats of Egidiu Pilastru's sheep, they had shot Teodosiu Bullica in the legs as a reminder, leaving him bedridden until his death.

From the Arvadas Boranzela had also inherited pride and scorn for danger. Until the age of twenty she remained frighteningly delicate and skinny, and looked as if she was starving to death. She made one meal a day, in the late afternoon. In the morning she drank only water from the well, accompanied by a spoonful of sugar, and the same again at lunch and supper time. When she sat down at the table, at about a quarter to six, she always ate the same thing, a sheet of *pane carasau*, a slice of casizzolu cheese, a raw egg and whatever fruit was in season. Apples were her favourite, particularly when they were still firm and sharp. She ate them whole, unpeeled, in great bites, spitting out only the seeds. Her aunts were obsessed with her eating habits.

'Eat a bit of meat and drink a glass of wine, it'll fatten you up and put some colour in your cheeks!'

She wouldn't hear of it. Eating meat struck her as a mortal sin.

And so it went on, until the day of the christening of Coseme Frighinias; she was godmother, with Lucianu Gardulinu as godfather. During the baptismal lunch, her new companion persuaded her to try a slice of wild boar prosciutto.

'Ajò, try it, it's the meat of a harmful creature, the Lord above won't say anything!'

Boranzela put it nervously into her mouth and didn't chew it immediately. She held it between tongue and palate and tried to suck it: it was sweet, and melted with her saliva like a piece of sugarloaf.

'So how is it? Good?'

She asked him to cut her a good slice, and ate it with bits of dried bread.

'Who made it?' she asked finally, as a glass of wine was poured for her.

'Ilariu Lathone, the poacher,' replied Lucianu.

After that christening meal, each time she saw the poacher Ilariu, Boranzela's mouth watered, she had strange dreams at night and woke up very agitated in the morning.

'*Mamma mia*, what's happening to me?' she wondered.

What was happening was that she had fallen in love and couldn't love, because she had vowed that her possessions would follow her to the grave:

'I'm not leaving anything to anyone! If the worst comes to the worst, I'll leave everything secretly to some stranger in Noroddile. The people of Abacrasta don't deserve so much as a glass of water!'

Her village and its inhabitants loathed her with a passion. She would rather have been born by the sea, where she could spend her time swimming like a fish and only leave the water to sleep. Out of desperation, to keep from giving herself to Ilariu, she started eating without restraint, and was soon as fat as a pig. Her clothes no longer fitted, and she couldn't even get into her shoes. Her eyes shrank, squashed into their orbits by her pink, ham-like cheeks. Her hands looked like round loaves, and she moved her legs without lifting them, almost sliding along the ground. From her shoulders to the beginning of her backside she looked like a metal vat, the kind they still use today for boiling up tomatoes to put in cans. Going to bed had become a huge exertion, and getting up a curse. She could no longer bend to go to the toilet, and when her period came her aunt had to apply her sanitary towels.

Her Aunt Lavretha was worried and told her so:

'Look at you, you're slowly committing suicide, Boranzelè! Take yourself in hand, or soon you won't be able to get through the front door!'

She didn't reply, having reached the point where she opened her mouth only to chew. Lest she exhaust her jaws, she had assumed the habit of eating only soft things: eggs beaten in marsala, puddings, mashed potatoes, bananas, dates, jam, chocolate, ricotta, honey, doughnuts, all kinds of soup. By the age of twenty-five she weighed a hundred and fifty kilos, the weight of a bullock ready for slaughter.

She went on having strange dreams at night, and in the morning her bed was always drenched with pink foam, as smooth and dense as shampoo. Her metal bedstead, which had buckled, had been replaced by a big table four inches thick. Rosedda, the maid who attended to her in the house in Sas Damas, where she had gone to live alone, also had to change her underwear and brush her hair.

By the age of forty-eight there wasn't a set of scales that could weigh her, not even the one at the chemist's. Weighing her naked, like an animal, Tziu Mialeddu Bistecca told her she now came in at nearly two hundred kilograms. The day came when she could no longer get up. She tried to straighten her back and sensed that an anvil was keeping her pressed to the mattress, so she started crying and called for a tray of cream cakes to console herself.

'Twelve of every kind!' she said to Rosedda.

She also started to grow a kind of blond fur, as short and soft as silk. She asked Tuniedda Pullache, a neighbour who used to visit her out of kindness, to bring her a man's razor and a box of blades.

'The more you shave it off, the more it will grow!' Tuniedda warned.

Boranzela was so insistent that there was nothing to be done.

In the last of her dreams, she was the goddess of the sea, falling from a rock into the arms of Ilariu Lathone. They swam together to a volcanic island, and each time they approached the shore a rain of fire drove them far back into the water. During that dream, the Voice emerged from the mouth of the volcano:

'Ajò! Ajò!'

On the morning that Rosedda found her with her wrists slit, the bedroom looked like a copper pot of blood. On one of the chests of drawers, in full view, she had left a sheet of paper written in an awkward, childish hand. It was her will. After the list of goods and money deposited at the bank and the post office, came the final note.

'In full possession of my faculties of intention and volition, I leave all this to Ilariu Lathone . . .'

That gesture ennobled Boranzela Coro 'e Cane more completely than even a lifetime spent doing good works

60

would have done. On the day of her funeral, everyone mourned her like a sister. I told my friends:

'Poor thing! Deep down she wasn't as horrible as she seemed. Perhaps she deserved a better death!'

10

Chilleddu Malevadau

Chilleddu Malevadau – 'the Wretch' – was born deaf, blind and dumb, three misfortunes in one, as if the mere fact of living were not already bad enough. His mother, Adelasia Galanzu, had taken a vow of virginity, in gratitude to Santa Lucia, who had restored her sight after an accident. At the age of thirteen, during the feast of her patron saint, she had been playing with the boys, who were lighting firecrackers and slipping them into the guttering pipes to cause explosions. She leapt about like a baby goat, laughed and showed off her new mother-of-pearl teeth. *Boom! Boom! Boom!*

Before she went home she asked for a firework from Giuvannicu Bitta, to set off on her own. She lit it with a match and slipped it into an empty bottle. *Boooom!* She had no time to get away. The bottle went off right in her face.

She was black as coal, and then the blood from the wounds made by the glass shards began to flow, making her face a mask of blood. She was picked up from the ground by some people from the neighbourhood of Melas Ruias, who cleaned her up as best they could. Her eyes were swollen, as burnt as potatoes cooked in hot coals. Gonaria Mulargia, who acted as her godmother, said to her through her tears:

'Oh, daughter of mine! Didn't you know that tears and laughter were close kin?'

She was blind for two years, until she was taken to the novena of Santa Lucia, to ask the saint for the miracle that the doctors had been unable to perform. They dressed her up in a pink tunic with a crown of bramble thorns, made her drink a decoction of dried mistletoe leaves and boiling water, and laid her at the base of the statue with her feet towards the door. After a quarter of an hour they made her stand up again and took her bandages off. From that moment she could see as before, as if nothing had happened. After a week her eyes had returned to the crystalline colour of the sky seen from the hill of Busellis.

The price she paid for the miracle was the promise of her virginity. She couldn't leave the saint unpaid, or fob her off with an act of charity. She had to give her something big, and in Abacrasta the poor women kept their capital hidden between their legs.

At the age of twenty-three, Adelasia Galanzu was so

beautiful that it would have been worth going to prison to have her. She had a whole street of admirers rich and poor. Keeping her vow was exhausting, and her nights were sleepless. Sometimes she craved to paint her lips and go out into the street, to give herself to the first man who came along. To cool her ardour, she washed with cold water whatever the season.

This lasted until the age of thirty, when fate laid its evil hand upon her once again. One evening one of her youngest brother's comrades-in-arms paid the family a visit, and when everyone had fallen asleep after dinner, the two of them went out into the courtyard to tell one another stories. Andria Cumida, for that was the name of the guest, who was originally from Melagravida, span her around and around like a chicken on a spit, and then took her into the woodshed. There they caught fire, and the inevitable happened. At the fatal moment, just as they finished devouring one another, a donkey brayed and woke up everyone in the neighbourhood.

'When the donkey brays the hay is ablaze!' was the saying in the village.

The damage was done. After a great ordeal of spitting and despair, and against the will of Adelasia's family, Chilleddu came into the world. Andria Cumida disappeared like a wisp of smoke and no one in Abacrasta ever saw him again.

Everyone, apart from the child's mother, saw the birth

as a curse. Some people would happily have taken those five pounds, six ounces of water made flesh by the will of God, and thrown it in the dustbin in a plastic sack or an empty feed-bag.

Chilleddu was born two months premature and looked like a skinned hare. Dark blood could be seen pulsing darkly beneath his pink skin, the rims of his eyelids creased into a sort of purple cockscomb; his tongue split at the tip like a fork; his auditory canal blocked by an olive-sized lump of cartilage like a coral earring.

'*Malevadau* – a wretch!' said the midwife who helped with the birth.

'A wretch!' said everyone who went to see him, moved less by pity than malevolent curiosity.

Adelasia's father, Veneriu Galanzu, fell ill and developed the habit of sleeping in the sheep-pen, giving the excuse that his fourteen-year-old servant shepherd had taken his own life.

'We can't leave the animals alone at a time like this!' he said. 'That's all we need – someone could steal our sheep, and then we'd be ruined completely!'

As far as he was concerned the sheep were more important than the child sent by fate to ruin his old age. Adelasia's mother, Maritria Thirrica, could do nothing but weep:

'The saints are angry with us! You've really done it now, my daughter, bringing this bastard into the world!'

For the people of Abacrasta it was as if the child had never been born, they saw him as a sin to be forgotten, a bad smell they hoped would disperse as quickly as possible.

In the end, tired of being treated like a dog with ringworm, Adelasia summoned the courage to leave home and moved to the neighbourhood known as Limbichìchinos, or the Place of the Stammerers. There she took a position as a maid with the Dunnales, a family of quarrymen who spoke more with their chisels than they did with their tongues.

In the neighbourhood of Limbichìchinos they were all like that, stuttering when they spoke, as if they had hot roast potatoes in their mouths all the time. They uttered their first few syllables in machine-gun bursts, but it took them a whole day to finish a sentence.

Adelasia didn't lose heart, after all, basically the same thing had happened to Our Lady, except that she had stayed a virgin and her child had been as lovely as the sun. Adelasia looked after a family of sixteen – Perseu and Filumena, the old ones, Tziu Eone Dunnales and Tzia Nicolosa Fughenti, and twelve children not counting her own.

The Dunnales, respecting the poor girl's misfortune and watching Chilleddu grow up without uttering a single word, felt like chatterboxes in comparison. The littlest children, when they were as young as four, prodded him with a shoemaker's awl and provoked him: 'Ajò, Chillè, speak! Are you deaf? Speak!'

Chilleddu couldn't even cry, those sharp pains assailed him from a hostile and mysterious darkness. With time, he had become used to recognising things and people by the touch of his hands. Sometimes the Dunnales were so mean that they made him touch things he shouldn't have touched, like shit or hot irons. The most malicious of them was Scilledda, one of the girls, who was fifteen years older than he and played him as a cat does a mouse.

Mamma Adelasia knew about all this, and she choked back her rage because there was no other way open to her: it was either this or death. A thousand times a day she thought of throwing herself into the Alenu river with her child clutched tightly in her arms. But the Voice hadn't called her, it had forgotten her, she had to pay for her sin by living, without the consolation of the rope.

Nonetheless Chilleddu, even though he had been punished by God at birth and then forgotten by mankind, grew up as strong as a young olive tree. At the age of nineteen he was strong enough to topple an ox to the ground, and had a lust for life that was the envy of Abacrasta.

After a night of exhaustion and terrible dreams, Adelasia decided to seek comfort in the fortune-teller Medea Telebis, and confided in her:

'Signora Medè,' she said, 'I can't bear my life any

longer. If things go on like this, my work will have finished me off before the Voice calls me!'

Signora Medea listened to her in silence, sipping from a glass of white altar wine and puffing hard on a Toscanello cigar. Finally she put her hand into her skirt pocket and took out a chicken's foot. She pulled three times on the white sinew that protruded from the shin, then said:

'Only he who has done you harm can take it away. I can't guarantee anything, because it isn't my way to pull the wool over people's eyes, but I advise you to return to the Sanctuary of Santa Lucia.'

Adelasia didn't need to be told twice. One day she asked for some time off, with the excuse that she was taking Chilleddu to a specialist in Noroddile and, taking him by the hand, she brought him to the sanctuary church. They walked there barefoot, crossing fields of grain and poppies, tearing the soles of their feet as they walked through the wild-lily brushwood, pursued by low clouds filled with wind and ancient fury.

Even though she was certain that her son couldn't hear her, Adelasia described the landscape with her voice. She told him of the flight of the bee-eaters, the song of the crickets, the sounding of the bells, the sleepy lament of the cuckoo:

'Look, Chillè . . . Listen, Chillè . . .'

She lent him the ears and eyes that she hadn't managed to give him at birth, she gave him a voice to express the wonder of all that was going on around them.

'We're there, Chillè. Chin up, my son.'

Thirty yards from the sanctuary, in the shadow of an oak tree, Adelasia saw a curious-looking blacksmith forging a golden net, as soft as a butterfly's wings but as tough as steel. It looked like the net of a sea horse fisherman. The blacksmith completed his task and turned to Adelasia and the boy:

'Give him this,' he said, 'it will make him more invulnerable than any armour could.'

The man disappeared in the sun's dazzling rays that danced among the thistles. Adelasia wrapped her son in the gold-threaded shawl, as they reached the front of the church. She pushed the heavy portal and went in. A pair of kestrels had nested in the saint's niche, from time to time the male swelled his red chest and moved his bluish tail like the pendulum of a wall clock. The female, hovering, beat her wings to protect her young.

Adelasia laid Chilleddu out beneath the altar, his feet towards the door, then knelt down and began to pray:

'Santa Lucia Virgin and Martyr, you alone can help me. I have suffered so much already for my sin. You who were condemned even though you were innocent, and who emerged from your shame with your head held high, intercede with God on behalf of this voiceless creature. Tell him that until today I have accepted from the Lord's hands all the harm he has done me. Tell him I can no longer endure the weight of grief, and beg him to grant a little serenity to these his feeble creatures. I am growing old, and my soul will never find consolation if I die before this wretched child of mine. Pray you do me the kindness of giving him back his health, or taking us both this moment!'

As she prayed, Adelasia felt a sudden chill, as if the weather had changed and the rain had started to fall. Yet coming to the doorway, she saw that the sun still scorched the earth, and its breath rose to the sky, making everything hazy. She went back inside and knelt down again to pray, facing Chilleddu. She touched his hands and they felt like ice. The floor of the church started to cover over with cold water that chilled her feet.

'My son! My son!' she started crying.

The water rose quickly, an inch a minute, and Chilleddu's body began to float. From the apse of the central nave, a white-painted piano that she had never seen before began to play a tune. Chilleddu stood up and began to dance, moving on enchanted feet to the waltzing sway. His gestures were filled with a deep and enchanting sense of peace. From the cracks in the wall there came the sound of staccato violins, brightly joining the notes of the piano.

Adelasia rubbed her eyes with the tips of her fingers: she was afraid that she was dreaming, afraid of going blind again. Her son, wet to the waist, bobbed over to his mother on the surface of the water and threw his arms around her neck:

70

'At last I can see you, my dearest mother! At last I can hear you!'

Adelasia nearly fainted and they fell together, floundering and laughing among the spray. Before they stepped out into the sun, Adelasia put a damp handkerchief over her son's forehead and brought it low over his eyes, so that the sun wouldn't burn them. When she looked at them, shading them with the palm of her hand, she discovered that her son had the most beautiful eyes in the world, they were watery and deep, like two sea marbles stolen from the bottom of the ocean. They sat down hand in hand on the curved stone benches in front of the church, and started to tell each other of their torments.

No one celebrated Chilleddu's miracle. Not the Bishop of Noroddile, nor the local newspapers, having other things to do. There were elections under way, the factory was beginning to smoke its toxic cigar over the plain, references to be sought by those wishing to work in the factory. There were rustic feasts to be organised, the Orotho feud was raging like a mistral wind. As far as the village was concerned, where the presence of Chilleddu Malevadau had once been merely irritating, now it had become awkward. The Lord had miscalculated once again.

Chilleddu would always be the illegitimate son of Adelasia and an outsider, was a cross to be borne to the top of the mountain, until his death.

'A bastard he will always be!'

71

'What do they think, that we're going to put him on the altar?'

Some people denied the truth of the past, saying that Chilleddu had been healthy at birth, that his mother had put a rag over his eyes and blocked his ears to get the invalidity benefit.

'Those wretched Galanzus would do anything for crooked money!'

Others said that Adelasia had become the lover of the eldest son of Eone Dunnales, to steal from him the little that he had.

'That toad-bag had loads more children, except she threw them down the black well!'

Those evil words forced Chilleddu and his mother to live in a cottage away from the dwelling they had inherited from Gonaria Mulargia, who had died without other heirs, sharing it with a cow and two goats. Before long, local soldiers had stolen the animals for a quick snack. So there were days when they were forced to eat raw potatoes seasoned only with salt. They lived in the direst poverty, as all around them everything burst with affluence, even the houses of the poor had fridges and televisions.

Chilleddu had tried hundreds of times to find a job. He was chased away as if he had the plague:

'What are we supposed to do with someone like you, hold you up as a saint? You've never learned to do anything!' they scoffed. 'We don't need a cripple, what we need is real men! Understand?'

Broken by despair, Chilleddu started losing weight until he was nothing but skin and bone. He drew less nourishment from bread than he did from his anger over the tricks that fate had played on him – twice now.

'You should have cracked me against the wall like a cat as soon as I was born!' he said to his mother.

Within the four walls of their hovel there was neither light nor water. When there was any food to be had, they cooked on a wood fire, otherwise they went to bed hungry after sharing a bit of fruit that they'd stolen from the fields. They never went down to Abacrasta any more, because the evil tongues down there were sharp as knives, and their very looks could kill.

One night when the moon was full, and a big white dove settled on the window ledge, Chilleddu heard the Voice calling him. He caught the dove, cut off its wings and flew to the holy wood of Sos Padentes, below Monte Isteddu. First, high in the sky, he flew three times over Abacrasta, raining little pieces of paper over the roofs and the streets. At Sos Padentes he settled on top of the most beautiful tree, under the branches of which full-grown lambs were sacrificed and roasted each year, for the feast of Santa Lucia. He took a piece of wire and moistened it with his saliva until the noose slipped easily, then off he flew, towards the unknown that he had already half explored. A violent jerk and his body snapped in two. His head, its sockets empty once again, fell into an abandoned goshawk's nest.

It was 1971 and I was playing as goalkeeper in the Abacrasta team at the top of the local league. I went to football training with one of the pieces of paper he dropped clutched in my fist, and I didn't read it until I was out on the field:

'In my weakness was my strength. Remember that. Chilleddu.'

11

The servant shepherd

Tziu Veneriu Galanzu's servant shepherd was called Candidu Vargia, the Swift, because his body was as slender as a bird's, his back a dark-brown, copper colour and his face was red. He looked as if he was born for the countryside, and since childhood he had spent much of his time with sheep. His gait was lithe and elegant, and no one could beat him at milking or *istrumpa*, not even the oldest shepherds.

The stories he told about the things that had happened to him were beyond belief. I always remember him with a smile, his eyes dancing with some strange, mysterious joy. He was only seven years older than me, but already he looked like a man. He wore a cloth beret at a rakish angle, wide-legged trousers and collarless shirts. I never saw him in a jacket or cape, even in winter, he obviously wasn't afraid of the cold. His eyes were black, two bits of burned-out coal nestled just below his forehead. His hands were like the shovels used by bakers to make *pane carasau*.

One morning he met me at the creamery door as I was chewing on a corner of bread still hot from the oven. He let his herd of sheep run on down the street and handed me a little lamb he was holding under his arm.

'Look after it well, because it's a twin and condemned to die. Its mother can't feed two. I'll bring you colostrum every evening on my way back from the sheep-pen.'

I still carry that lamb and Candidu Vargia's eyes like a treasure in my heart. He brought me colostrum in a tin jerrycan for forty days, until the lamb was weaned, and then, the same evening that my parents cut the lamb's throat to roast it, Candidu went up to the Mariane Zori vineyard and did some work on the gate. It was New Year's Eve, 1949, and less than a week had passed since my grandfather's death. Two periods of mourning so close together in time had convinced me that big celebrations brought more misery than amusement.

Everyone envied Candidu Vargia's vivacity, which was such that he could never stand still, and always had to be on the move – even when he should have stayed put.

'He has quicksilver in his veins!'

'He'll stop leaping around soon enough when they fry him in his own oil!' they said in Abacrasta.

In 1936, the year of his birth, it is said that there was a

76

terrible famine in the village, after locusts devastated the crops. That year the locusts were joined by lice, as big as grains of corn and hungry as dogs. You couldn't get the lice out of your hair even with napthaline, and the men's balls were rubbed raw from scratching with their nails. That was why Candidu was forever leaping about. Don Zigarru even made everyone take part in a religious procession, with Santa Lucia and the Saint of the Harvest at their head. All in vain! Prayers and holy water merely fattened the creatures.

In the end the inhabitants of Abacrasta were forced to put into practice the advice of Dr Poddighe, a man from the coast who knew more about insects than he did about people. They brought a hundred copper cauldrons into the Piazza di San Bernardino and arranged them in a circle on iron tripods. They filled them with water and ashes, piled dry arbutus branches onto the fire and got out their matches.

The old people still speak of that event as a great one. People stripping off in public to cleanse themselves in the caustic mixture. The women bringing clothes, blankets and sheets from their houses to disinfect them in the boiling fluid. Children crying and coming out of the pots as pink as piglets. The most manly of the men shamelessly stripping off their underpants, and the others covering their wretchedness with their hands. The women staying in their shifts lest they incite the drunkards. Don Zigarru being stripped by force and threatening excommunication. And rivers of wine and brandy, baskets of puddings, music and dancing.

No one ever knew for sure why the lice and locusts went away. Perhaps Tziu Pietrinu Dindillu, still alive and healthy, knows the answer:

'Those beasts saw how mad we all were, and took to their heels!'

Tziu Pietrinu may not be far wrong when he says how weird and unpredictable we are, like a bunch of arses who can't find a place to sit. At the age of ten, Tziu Veneriu Galanzu had taken Candidu into the country as a favour to his father, who couldn't bear the child's constant movement, and because Galanzu needed someone to sleep in the sheep-pen and look after his sheep.

Candidu quickly learned to milk the sheep and make cheese. He got on better with animals than with people. If one of them began to limp, developed a fever or suffered from mastitis, he could tell as much from its eyes and set it apart from the others to treat it. His secret medicine was an infusion of various herbs: pellitory, nettles, mallow, hemlock.

Candidu spent the best years of his short life on Tziu Veneriu's land, chasing the clouds that floated in the sky, taking the ram by the horns, doing his business in the open air, picking off his lice in the heat of the sun. In his four years in the countryside, whether for reasons of age or family, no

78

one had ever treated him harshly. He had never lost a sheep, never fallen out with any of his fellow shepherds.

Three bandits from Taculé came one night to ruin his life, taking away fifty lambs destined for the slaughter. Candidu, poor fellow, had gone to sleep exhausted and had not noticed a thing. Tziu Veneriu Galanzu grew fiercer than his dogs, tore into Candidu and thrashed him with the cattle whip. The last blow landed on his face, breaking his teeth and opening up a long cut at the corner of his mouth.

'A curse be upon you! You've let them rob you of a year's work! Bastard! Who's going to pay me now, eh? Are you going to go to the thieves and right the wrong? And I thought you were a man!'

Tziu Veneriu had never been like that before. Clearly he was good at concealing his irascible side. While everything had gone well, he had treated Candidu almost like a son: a pair of leather shoes every year, plenty of food, a sheep registered in his name every three months, the occasional drop of thick red wine.

Candidu, out of respect for his elders, didn't react, but bore the blows and the insults in silence. Then he ran back to his father's house, still bleeding and in tears, and begged his father to find him another master, because if he stayed with Tziu Veneriu he feared he might do something stupid.

'I'll kill him, Papa! If you make me go back I'll wring his neck with my bare hands!'

As if Candidu had not had enough already, his father added further blows and insults:

'And who are you going to kill, you little sod! If you'd stayed awake, the whole thing would never have happened! You just trot right back to the sheepfold and apologise!'

Candidu pretended to obey and went to wash in the tub in the courtyard. The Voïce came, sudden and shrill, from the rusty, dripping water pipe. Before he left he went into the stable and took the rope that bound the donkey to the iron ring. With the rope wrapped around his chest, he went straight to the vineyard owned by his uncle Vittorinu.

There, out of spite for the bandits, he hanged himself from the gate and lost his wager with death.

12

Tragasu Imbilicu

The gravedigger Tragasu Imbilicu said the same thing every time he saw me:

'Hey Battì! Don't forget to keep a space for me in the death register. Part Two, Series B, please!'

He talked about his imminent death as if he was staring it in the face. And he laughed, showing jagged teeth and a scar that had divided his skull in two like a deep crevasse.

'Get ready, Battì! Get ready!'

One winter some years ago he had fallen from a black fig tree, in the fields at Sos Prideddos. He was rushed to hospital, where he spent seventy days in a reversible coma. They couldn't open up his head, because a blood clot had coagulated in some impossible corner. When he returned to the land of the living, and the people of Abacrasta asked him spitefully about his accident, he told them:

'Who knows! I was picking figs and all of a sudden, thump! I'm on the ground. That's all I can remember.'

'And in hospital, Tragà, what was it like? What did you see when you were in a coma?'

'I didn't see a thing! I was happy as a rock. No pain, nothing to worry about!'

In Abacrasta even the children knew there were no ripe figs in January, and that Tragasu Imbilicu had had something else in mind when he climbed the tree. His drinking companions, to conceal his shame, had got rid of the rope, cut to measure and with the noose all ready.

Tragasu had no close relations in the village. The ones that weren't lying five feet under in the Truncos Malos cemetery had all emigrated, some to the mainland, others scattered at random throughout the world. None of them dropped him a line to ask him how he was, confirming that no one gave a tuppenny damn about his life.

His father and mother had disappeared in the year of the great snow, when the earth had been covered for four months and the sun had been kidnapped by darkness. They were never found, either dead or alive. There was only one credible hypothesis: the Voice. Not even the vilest bandit would have attempted to blackmail them, because they had more debts than hairs on their heads. They couldn't have had any bills to settle for land or animals, because they owned nothing but the clothes on their backs.

Love affairs could not have come into it, because Tzia Gesuina was toothless, with more wrinkles on her face than a prune, and Tziu Bartolomeu stank of piss and cigars from half a mile away.

Tziu Bartolomeu Savuccu was so lazy that he wouldn't even bend down to pick up money from the floor. He used to spend his time walking up and down the main street of the village, staring at the cobbles as if he had lost something and spewing out swirls of dense smoke that smelled of overcooked liver and fried onions.

'The land swallowed them up before the snow melted!' people said, and there was an end to it.

When he was left an orphan, Tragasu was four years old. He owned a wooden spinning-top, two pairs of patched-up trousers, a shirt, two vests, a sweater, a pair of worn-out shoes, a brazier, a piss-pot, three forks, three spoons, three enamel plates, a saucepan, a frying pan and two turtle doves in a wooden cage. The house where the family lived, and all the furniture in it, belonged to Tziu Battore Crastu, who, when Mama Gesuina was late paying the rent, took payment in kind.

They had lived in the neighbourhood of Sos Poetas, a long, blind alley like a pig's gut, with a drinking fountain against the end wall, a little food shop on the right, a bar on the left, and a channel down the middle to catch the families' effluent.

Tragasu was put in an orphanage in Noroddile run by

nuns. For years he ate nothing but boiled cabbage, powdered milk, stale cheese, mildewed jam, yesterday's bread. In that sort of children's home nothing was fresh, everything smelled stale including the nuns, who had beards like men.

Five times Tragasu escaped from Our Lady's House of Refuge, and on each occasion he was caught and brought back. Once he secretly boarded a bus for the sea: that was a great day. Bracing air, water that foamed as if it was fizzy, happy children chasing a kite as big as a real falcon, people eating under parasols, and waves, lots of waves that billowed over one another like days long gone. One died on the next without leaving a trace, just a long *spliisshh*.

Things changed when he was adopted by the old grave-digger of Abacrasta, Tziu Mario Sunza, known as Baule, or Trunk. He brought him home to please his wife, a dried-up womb who couldn't have children. Little by little he taught him all the tricks of the trade, and finally recommended him to the mayor's office as his successor.

Tragasu had tried long and without success to find a wife. A man with a job like that wasn't the kind to take to your bed and start a family with. Most likely he would have talked about nothing but headstones, memorial pictures and epitaphs. To compensate, he bought a bicycle with his first money, and rode that, instead of chasing after women. As he came down from the cemetery he flew like the wind. *Svyooom, svyooom*. He had also got hold of a cap made of strips of leather and a pair of dark glasses. From a distance he looked like a real cyclist, one of the ones who darted along the road when the Giro d'Italia passed the crossroads by the Abacrasta roadman's house.

For that occasion, Tragasu put on his jersey, his cycling shoes and shorts, and mingled with the racers. The peasants mockingly applauded him:

'Come on, Traga, you're in the lead! Show those amateurs some dust! Show them who you are!'

He was sweating and his lungs were about to explode and then, just past the first bend, when everyone was out of sight, he threw himself to the ground and wept. He went to the black fig tree, the one where he used to do his business, with two sheets of newspaper in his pocket and a cigarette stub in his mouth. Before climbing up it he had thought long and hard.

'I've lived a fool, and I'll die a fool,' he had repeated to himself for months in his lonely house.

After his unsuccessful suicide attempt he felt a pang of guilt. The whole time he had been in a coma not a single person in Abacrasta had died. He became convinced that he was a jinx, a bird of ill-omen, a harbinger of doom. Even when he was born, on a night with a full moon following the summer solstice, he was told that the barn owl had hooted for ages in the forest.

When the Voice called him for a second time, lest he make another mistake he bought himself a drawing pad and, with his pencil, he began to plan his journey into the land of the dead. He made a lot of sketches and chose the one that seemed the best. Without making a great show of it, he bought a chestnut coffin from Tziu Nespula and set to work. First he dug the hole, excavating earth by the spadeful. Then he lowered in the coffin and opened the lid. He planted two posts at the side, and a platform made of planks that he had nailed together. He piled the earth on top of the platform. He wiped the sweat from his forehead, drained a bottle of wine and dropped into the hole. It was hellishly hot, and the earth smelt of cut roots and melting chocolate.

He stretched himself out in the coffin, with the lid ready to snap shut. To bring the earth sliding down all at once, he had tied two rope ends to the poles and knotted them to the wrist of his right hand. He closed his eyes and tugged hard. *Shhhlooompf*. As he slowly finished his last breath, he saw the sea once more, heard the voices of the children running after the kite, felt the foam splashing his feet, the wave carrying him away for ever. *Shhhlooompf*. Then nothing, just a sound like a lorry unloading sand. From the whitewashed dome of the church the startled crows took flight towards the gorge of Mutzugolai.

In the empty space on the twenty-fifth page of the death register, Part Two, Series B, I wrote the name of Tragasu Savuccu, known as Imbilicu, with a heavy heart.

I neglected to say that he was so-called because

whenever he ate too much his belly swelled up like a leather bottle, and his belly button – *imbilicu*– stood out like the dentate leaf of a navelwort.

Part Two

Of Life Regained and
Other Stories

13

Micheli Isoppe

The blind woman Redenta Tiria knocked again and again at
Micheli Isoppe's door. *Tap, tap, tap, tap* . . . No one
replied, the house seemed to be uninhabited. The red
carnations that grew in big tins hanging from the wall,
filled the air with their sharp scent. Redenta walked along
the wall and plucked one. First she sniffed it greedily, then
slipped it into her hair. The scarlet flower looked like a
bright sun in the mantle of the night.

Tap, tap, tap, tap . . . The angular shadows of the walls
fell steeply into the street, bouncing off the tarmac, which
had been softened by the sun. Redenta lifted the spoon-
handle latch and walked in. Although the blind woman
couldn't see it, the courtyard was shaped like a horse-shoe.
On the right, covered by a corrugated iron roof, were the
forge, the anvil, a long iron table, the press, hammers,

clubs, mallets, pincers, hacksaws and a new soldering iron, barely used. The grey walls were stained with a crystalline metallic soot, cobwebs and dark dust everywhere. Two chickens scratched at a pile of wood shavings. Hanging from the walls were compasses, callipers, disembowelled alarm clocks and a collection of big old keys. On the left were piles of iron rods, tin cans, sheets of metal, an icon of Santa Lucia, a palm leaf plaited with an olive twig, chains, cartwheels, skeins of wire, a dog and a bay horse. The two animals were so thin that it was hard to tell them apart.

In the middle stood a persimmon tree that had dropped a carpet of sharp fruit. They still fell down from time to time, as if to stress the transience of life. Next to the façade of the house there was a flowerbed with various kinds of large plants, all dehydrated and bearing withered flowers. On the step by the glass door leading into the kitchen, a mongrel cat licked its tail.

'Michè! Micheli!'

In a niche above the door stood a featureless plaster Madonna and a glass jar of dry lilies.

'Micheli! Are you there?'

No one replied. Redenta pushed the door with her toe and found herself in the kitchen. Four chairs, their cushions eviscerated by the cat, a table with many layers of varnish but no particular colour, a pair of broken glasses, dirty dishes, a plate-rack, the fridge, a television with a built-in aerial, some piles of pornographic magazines, Mickey Mouse comics, clock-making journals, dirty clothes thrown on the floor, empty bottles stained with dark wine.

'Oh Michè!'

Nothing. From the adjacent room, separated off by a greasy cretonne curtain, there came the sound of someone's wheezing breath. Redenta took a few silent steps and held the curtain aside with her hand. Micheli Isoppe was standing naked on a chair, with his belt tied around his neck and fixed to one of the rings on the pole used for hanging big pork sausages. A long beard, wild eyes, lost in their effort to extract a good memory from life. He had already bent his leg for a kick to say goodbye to the world.

Redenta didn't say anything, she just returned his gaze with her blind eyes. He closed his own eyes and felt suddenly giddy. In a swirling merry-go-round of amber horses he saw all the faces of the people who had shaped his life. His sweat-drenched mother taking the bread from the mouth of the oven, his father with his leather apron, beating the hot iron, his sister who had left for the mainland in search of her fortune, his brother who had donned an army uniform to earn his livelihood, Pierina who had given him his first kiss and then married Manuelle Tivazza, Pippinu Muschitta who had poked him in the eye after a game of *morra*, his grandmother who had blown on the coffee spoon to cool it down so that he could taste it, his

93

grandfather who brought home blackberries in a cabbage leaf, Cleopatra, the whore who emptied his cauldron of despair every Saturday.

That was where his life began and ended. There had never been anything else of any importance except the *bam, bam* of the hammer striking the anvil, measuring out his days. It was true that he had started building a kind of time machine, but it had brought him only sadness, adding loneliness to loneliness. He had designed it as a boy, when he had been wild about clockwork mechanisms, and built it as a grown-up, investing all his savings in it.

From Tziu Castanza, an old clockmaker in Noroddile, he had bought all kinds of clocks, wall clocks, alarm clocks, pendulum clocks. He had got it into his head that he could reverse time, make it go backwards. Since finding a table clock in the attic, he had taken to looking up the subject in the library. The first money his father gave him he spent on specialised journals: *Clocks and Me*, *Time and Us*, *The Modern Hour-Glass*, *The Diapason*, *In Search of Lost Time*.

His idea was as simple as it was useless: if oscillatory motion could be transformed into intermittent rotation, why, rather than making it go forwards, could it not be made to go backwards? He had forgotten that he was born in Abacrasta, where people have their clocks within them, and only the Voice decides when they should stop.

But Micheli Isoppe was as hard and stubborn as the iron he worked. He spent his time fiddling with springs, gearwheels, weights, spirals, crowns, balances. The hours flowed over him, as heavy and sticky as bitter honey.

In the end he had managed to build a gadget that rather resembled a sports car. He had sat down in the driver's seat and pulled a lever, waiting to return to his childhood. He sat there like that for three days, without eating or drinking. Eventually, he faced facts, because he wasn't stupid, and since then he had preferred to spend his time flicking through porn mags, waiting for the Voice.

Micheli opened his eyes. Redenta was still standing in front of him. He loosened the noose and slipped it from his head. The woman approached him, gave him her hand and helped him down.

'Who are you? Why did you come?' asked Micheli Isoppe.

'I am the daughter of the sun and I have come to bring light into the land of shadows,' replied Redenta.

'But you're blind, how can you be the daughter of the sun?'

'Because my father blinded me as a little girl, by loving me too much.'

'And how did you get here?'

'He guided me, he who hates human sacrifice. Go, he told me, and stop those wretches of Abacrasta who no longer wish to enjoy my light!'

When the blind woman left Micheli Isoppe, everything

in the courtyard and in the rooms was clean and tidy, as though an invisible wife had been working for forty days. The time machine had disappeared, and on his unmade bed there was the smell of carnations and a lock of raven hair.

Within a few months the blacksmith had found companionship and began to share the *bam, bam* of the hammer on the anvil with Paskedda Tivazza, the widow Murisca.

14

Serafina Vuddi Vuddi

Serafina Vuddi Vuddi – her nickname meant 'Bubbling Pot' – was the most famous prostitute of the province. Her real surname was Raspitta. She sold herself in Noroddile, in a room at the foot of Monte Nofre, with saints on the walls and a wardrobe crammed with clothes from market stalls, and love-stories in photographs. Two long candles were always lit on the chests of drawers. Shepherds and civil servants, shopkeepers and students had all been between her legs.

Once the bishop had even paid her a visit, in a bid to bring her back to the flock. Rather than money, he had given her a phosphorescent plastic rosary and a ticket for the cinema.

'Pray, my daughter! Pray!' he had said. 'Pray for me and for you, because we both give ourselves to our neighbour for no real reason!'

Bishop Trabbis hadn't a clue. Serafina had a thousand and one reasons to give herself to others. The first and the most important of these was money. She wanted to put a great deal aside to make sure her old age was better than her childhood, which had been torture.

She was born in Gospotolò, a village twenty miles from the sea, no mountains or hills, just a heel of land rising like an overturned goblet on the plain. Dogs and wind, broad beans and heat. The only decent thing in the place was the River Tisamene, with its black-stained green frogs, beautiful to look at and delicious to eat, sunbathing on the stones; with its dark, delicate and carnivorous damselflies; with its pond-skaters jumping and diving in the pools of stagnant water; the pink flowers of love-lies-bleeding, apparently trying to touch the sky; the swarms of chrysalids waiting for June to take flight. Serafina would go to the river with her dog. Often she would sit down on the bank and throw pieces of wood that were carried away by the current.

'Fetch, Ruffi! Fetch!'

The dog obeyed like a servant, took the stick in its mouth and brought it back to her, whining with pleasure. Sometimes, with a touch of cruelty, she would throw the odd pebble onto the water, too.

'Fetch, Ruffi! Fetch!'

Ruffi came back to the shore tired and disappointed, dangling his steaming tongue and angrily shaking the water from his back. To scare him and make him even more obedient, she yelled at him in a loud voice:

'Bad dog, Ruffi! Bad dog!'

Ruffi lay down and yelped until Serafina stroked him between the ears.

There was nothing in Gospotolò, not a school or a church. It was part of the municipality of Santa Maria, and anyone who wanted to learn to read or make a confession had to travel three miles on foot or on the back of a donkey. Even to be buried you had to go to the cemetery in Santa Maria.

As soon as she finished school she spent three years at a teachers' training college in Olospia, before dropping out. From that day onwards Serafina started fighting with her mother. She addressed her like an ill-mannered boy; reproaching her from dawn till dusk for bringing her into the world.

'A fine place you've brought me into! Find me a job in Noroddile, because I don't want to spend another day in this place! I'll be a servant if that's what you want, just get me out of here!'

It hardly ever rained in Gospotolò. The sky grew dark, the clouds passed low and then went elsewhere, carried off by the warm wind. There were days when it looked as if you could touch them with your hands. Serafina went out on to the balcony and tried to catch them with the net she used to catch the river frogs.

One evening the sky turned as red as her first period, and the next day it began to rain as no one in those parts had ever seen it rain before. And with the rain, Signora Paulina came to Gospotolò. She was one of the beautiful daughters of Don Grazianu Murcione, the richest man in Noroddile. She had recently married Professor Piattu, head of the surgical department at the San Giovanni Hospital, and was looking for a girl to keep her company and take care of things in the house.

For Serafina it was like seeing the Madonna herself. Signora Paulina stepped out of her car and knocked at the first door in the village, which happened to be Serafina's. It was summer, and Paulina was wearing a wine-yellow silk suit, with a wide-brimmed straw hat that shaded her face to the eyebrows. Her eyes were sage-green, matching her high-heeled shoes and her handbag. She was so beautiful that she didn't look real.

'Excuse me, where does Tomasina Berrules live?'

Serafina looked at her open-mouthed.

'She lives in this street, but she isn't here at the moment. She's gone to Santa Maria to sell curds at the market. She might be back after lunch.'

Mama Chischedda appeared behind her like a shadow:

'Is this how to treat people, Serafi, leave them standing at the door? Come in, young lady, come in! You don't want to be standing outside in weather like this.'

Signora Paulina replied politely, 'I'm sorry, but I can't, my husband's waiting for me in the car.'

'Then bring him in, too, and I'll make you a nice cup of coffee!'

Such insistent hospitality persuaded Signora Paulina to call her husband.

'Angelino, come in for five minutes, the girl we're looking for isn't here!'

The surgeon got out of the car, and when he saw Serafina he nearly had a heart attack. She reminded him of his first love at school, a certain Giuditta Contrio, who had died after falling from a horse. The same colour hair, like a ripe prickly pear, the same dark eyes, the same melodious voice that caressed your ear-drums, vampire lips that gleamed with a hint of pearly pink.

'And what nice things bring you to these parts?' Tzia Chischedda asked, her curiosity fired.

'We're looking for a trustworthy girl to work in our house, to attend to minor tasks, but most of all for company, because my husband's always at the hospital.'

Serafina sat up in her chair.

'And have you found her?'

'People in Noroddile recommended this girl Tomasina Berrules . . . they say the women of Gospotolò are unmatched on the island for honesty and diligence. Is it true?'

'It's true! It's true!' replied Serafina's mother. 'The women around here don't have bees in their bonnets, they don't watch television, they think only of work and the family.'

Angelo Piattu looked at Serafina and saw Giuditta Contrio, his great love, lost because of a runaway horse. Tzia Chischedda smiled, resting a hand on her daughter's shoulder:

'Hey! If you want, take this one, she's always making my head spin about wanting to go and work in Noroddile.'

Husband and wife looked at one another for a moment. They had barely walked into the house, and already they felt right at home with this woman, who was making their life so easy for them.

'Is what your mother says true?'

'Why would I lie to you?' Serafina replied, blushing.

'It might work out,' added Signora Paulina, 'as long as poor Tomasina doesn't mind.'

'I've already thought of that,' answered Tzia Chischedda. 'She's not the kind to dwell on things.'

They drew up an agreement about food, lodging, clothes and a few lire a month and two days later Serafina left Santa Maria on the seven o'clock bus. She was accompanied to the stop by her father, Tziu Bertu Raspitta, he with mule and suitcase and she on foot, wearing her new clothes bought from a mail-order catalogue, and a pair of white coral earrings, a present from her godmother. She would turn eighteen on the fifteenth of September, the day of Our Lady of Sorrows.

Before saying goodbye, her father hugged her and said, 'Love those who love you, and respond to those who love you! Remember that, Serafi!'

The words were meaningless, it was just a proverb that Bertu Raspitta had read the evening before in Frate Indovino's almanac. But Serafina liked it anyway. He could have said anything at all, because she was about to sprout wings and fly from Gospotolò, never to return.

Serafina reached the house of the Piattu-Murciones one morning when the sky was playing at raining and then suddenly stopping again. A quick splash on the houses and then nothing, as if someone, in the pauses in between, planned to soap the town and give it a good wash. As soon as the fiery eye of the sun appeared, people closed up their umbrellas, and a few minutes later down came the rain again.

Serafina's hair was rat-tailed by the showers, as she walked with her fake leather suitcase in one hand, a soaked piece of paper bearing the address in the other: 12, Via Monsignor Conchedda. The damp streets smelled of engine oil and fresh cabbages. Every now and again the smell of drains rose up from the manhole covers.

She walked past churches on either side and, finally, past a traffic policeman with a decorated beret and a clean uniform who offered to drive her.

'Where are we going?' asked Serafina when she noticed that they were already outside the town and the council car was climbing a tree-lined hill.

'First I wanted to show you the landscape from up at the top,' replied the traffic policeman. 'Have you been to Noroddile before?'

'Twice,' she said, 'the first time to visit someone in hospital, the second to see the August parade.'

'Ha, then you have lots of things to discover! How old are you?'

'I'll be eighteen in September.'

'And where are you from?'

'Gospotolò.'

'And what are you going to do at Signora Murcione's house?'

'I'm going to be a servant, a maid, in fact.'

Serafina started to feel a strange trembling in her legs, like when she got very tired on the way back home from the River Tisamene, with her dog running behind her.

From that moment onwards the traffic policeman didn't open his mouth again. He parked the car in a dip and made her get out, into a field littered with bits of tarpaulin, contraceptives and paper handkerchiefs. Dirty flowers damp with tears of rain. Serafina put her hand in her pocket to find the picture of her dog that one of her cousins had taken. At that moment, the policeman unbuttoned his

104

flies and said, 'I bet you don't get ice-creams like this in Gospotolò!'

To buy her silence, on the way back, he put three one-thousand lire notes in her hand. Dropping her by the Piattu-Murciones' porch, he looked at her menacingly before shutting his car door.

'Just you bear in mind that in Noroddile girls who do that kind of thing are lower than chicken-shit! You get me? So just you keep your trap shut!'

Serafina rang the bell and started unwrapping a honey-flavoured sweet, one of the ones her mother had given her to console her in times of discouragement. She sucked it twice and spat it out: it was bitter and tasted like a prickly persimmon.

The door was opened to her by Signora Paulina. She was holding a little dog, which was smaller than a rabbit and dressed like a baby.

'Oooh! Welcome to our humble abode!' she said in a tone partly affected, partly teasing. 'You'll soon see that you'll be right at home here!'

Serafina didn't speak, it was as if she was paralysed. The little dog barked at her.

'Don't be so shy! I can assure you we've never eaten anyone. Come in and I'll show you the house and your room!'

Signora Paulina put the dog on the ground and pushed the door shut.

Serafina spent twenty-three months, four days and one hour shut away in that prison, with Professor Piattu quickly robbing her of the treasure she kept between her legs, and Signora Paulina ordering her about with a rod of iron. The evening when Signora Paulina forced her to come into the bath-tub 'to give her a good soaping', she didn't sleep in her bed. The husband was bad enough, pulling down her knickers every blessed day, with the excuse that she reminded him of his first love, Giuditta Contrio.

As soon as Sabazio, a mechanic who took her to the pizzeria on Sundays, found her a room below the church of Santu Nofre, she set up on her own, and soon she had more clients than a doctor.

'Whore or no whore, at least I'm well paid!' That became her motto.

The rumour spread like lightning that a girl from Gospotolò, beautiful, young and cheap, had opened up shop in Via Ulimu Siccu, between a dairy and a greengrocer's.

'They've opened a fresh-meat shop!' they said.

'Any good?'

'Finest fillet, me old mate! Finest fillet!'

The village of Gospotolò, Serafina's parents and the rest of her family wiped her from their memory, cutting her off cleanly as you might an irritating wart. She worked honestly for twenty-seven years and then, to spend her old age in peace, she finally moved to Abacrasta.

She had been brought to the three-storey house near Sos Molentes by Damianu Zicoria, a landowner whose face was disfigured by a malignant tumour. On his left cheek, between his eye and the bridge of his nose, there was what looked like a bunch of bitter-tasting grapes, which changed colour from one day to the next, from dark red to purple to putrid green.

Damianu was frightening to look at, but he had a good soul and a big heart. The last time he paid a business visit to the room with the saints and burning candles, he made his suggestion to Serafina:

'Why don't you give it up? Come and stay in Abacrasta, and live like a lady! No one would dare offend you or lay a hand on you – if they do they'll have this to reckon with!' and he showed her the pistol he carried in his belt, behind his back.

She thought for a while, sitting on the edge of her bed, with her elbows on her knees and her chin cupped between her palms.

'If you don't make your mind up today, you'll end up paying men to come to bed with you! Do you think beauty lasts for ever?'

Damianu was right. Serafina's hips had grown heavy, her thighs were wrinkled like discarded cork bark, her breasts were soft as balloons filled with warm water. She thought about it for a week, then made her decision. She loaded bag and baggage into Damianu's estate car and off they went.

After a few years in Abacrasta, Serafina felt as if she'd been reborn. She thought she was in heaven. No one, not even Damianu, had ever told her anything about the Voice. They had a wedding with lots of guests, hosted a party that went on all day and received hundreds of little good-luck notes wishing them sons. To make her happy, her husband had also given her a maid and bought an Alfa Spider, a convertible.

'Hello, Signora Zicò! How are you, Signora Zicò?'

She was just like one of us, born here and baptised with water from the ancient well. But Serafina wasn't stupid, she had learned what men are like when they think they're strong and really they're weak. On her sprung mattress they were all the same, good and meek as kittens. Then, back outside, they turned back into the same old dogs they'd been before, with all their hypocrisy, greed, wickedness and envy. Behind the outward show, it pained her to discover that there lay the keen-edged malice of the heirs of Eracliu Palitta and Artemisa Crapiolu.

How stupid she had been, failing to see that when they had been wishing her sons. What sort of sons could she have at her age, with her belly tanned like a sheepskin and the muscles of her womb so flabby from her trade? Beneath the surface, people were spitting poison.

'Hah! Now even old whores with other people's property are coming back as virgins!'

'To see her coming into church like a saint! Has she no shame?'

'Couldn't Damianu have found anyone better?'

'And who would have taken him, my dear woman, with that illness of his?'

Serafina felt the voices piercing her skin like hot needles. She threw herself clumsily down, reflecting that there wasn't a square inch of healthy soil on her island. Noroddile, Gospotolò, Abacrasta, the whole world was the same, everyone was treacherous. But who would want her now? Not even the nuns at the rest home would take her in.

One afternoon when she was driving through Damianu's land she saw a goshawk in the sky and stopped to follow its flight. It hovered before darting straight down on its prey. For a moment she felt like a mouse, a hare, a weasel, a chicken, a snake. She turned on the stereo and kept her finger on the button, searching for a station at random. She needed music, any music but the whistle of the wind or the goshawk's cry. The little red light stopped at number fifty, her age.

She looked at herself in the rear-view mirror and saw that she was old. Without noticing, she had speeded up the tempo of her life, making her face look thirty years older than it really was. She noticed with irritation the first grey locks that wouldn't be defeated by dyes, the bags under her eyes as heavy as the suitcase of her first journey, her cheeks ballasted by the regrets that dragged her down, saggy as flannel.

The radio crackled like a piece of burning bacon. All of a sudden, out of the brown mesh of the speakers came the Voice:

'Ajò! Get ready, for your time has come!'

After that there came the sound of the saxophone solo from an old song she had listened to as a girl:

'Petite fleur, oh, my little flower . . .'

She opened the glove compartment. Beneath the papers and a map of the island she found the 7.5 calibre with the number filed off, which Damianu made her carry for protection:

'On our country roads you never know. There's always a chance of a dangerous encounter, and this thing here resolves problems faster than words.'

That was what Damianu had said to her, before teaching her to assemble and reassemble the gun, to load and cock the gun faster than a *carabiniere*. *Click, clack, click, clack*. It was like a toy, with all those bullets gleaming like gilded sugared almonds.

'If you need it, use it, fire! Don't take it out just to show it off, because if you do they'll know you're scared and grab it out of your hand. OK?'

In her life as a prostitute, Serafina had always needed to understand other people, that had been the most important thing. But wasn't there a better way of living, without any sort of understanding, like animals and trees? She picked up the pistol and weighed it in the palm of her right hand.

'My! It feels heavier than usual!' She brought the mouth of the barrel to her temple. 'Boom! And that's it! It's easier than having the dentist take a molar out!' she thought, to give herself courage.

She stroked the trigger with the tip of her index finger and released the safety catch. The bullet was already in the barrel. She checked to make sure no one was around. Behind her, in the ditch, a barefoot woman with long raven hair was running very quickly. Serafina put the gun back in the glove compartment, but didn't have time to close it.

'Can you give me a lift to Abacrasta?' asked Redenta Tiria.

'Sure!' stammered Serafina.

'I think I'm lost and I can't find my way.'

'Aren't you blind?'

'That's what they say!' replied Redenta, settling into the seat beside her. 'Although I know lots of people who are blind even though they can see perfectly well.'

There was a short pause. The goshawk was back in the air, circling above the car.

'So, shall we go?'

111

Serafina turned the key in the ignition.

At that moment, Redenta took the gun from the glove compartment and threw it into the thistles.

'Real people don't need those. Evil can't be given or taken away by gunfire. Remember that from now on!'

Serafina felt disoriented for a moment, unsure whether to reply or stay silent, stop the car or change gear.

'Go on, go on! We have a long journey ahead of us, and lots of things to talk about.'

Serafina put the car into gear and released the handbrake with a snap. The Spider sped along the road, lifting up dust and straw in its wake. They drove around, far and wide, for days, stopping only to fill up and buy things to eat, sleeping beneath the stars, and talking, talking, talking. Oropische, Orotho, Ispinarva, Piracherfa, Taculè, Melagravida, Thilipirches; they reached the sea of Pasadinas.

Neither you nor I may know what they talked about. The only sure thing is that Serafina Raspitta, known as the Bubbling Pot, returned to Abacrasta from that journey beautiful and resplendent as a sunflower. It was as if the gods had immersed her in a tub full of liquid light. In a cardboard box she brought back with her was a little silverberry plant, black soil still attached to its roots. She planted it in her courtyard and never allowed a living soul but Damianu near her little tree.

Two months later she knew she was pregnant, and gave

birth in May. She had the baby at home, in the old style, without letting any doctors get their hands on her; too many of them had defiled her in the past. She was assisted by Mintonia, the maid, who had seen some children born and others die. Damianu waited in the courtyard, his head turned towards the sun and his fingers united in prayer.

'Let him be healthy and well! That's all I ask, oh Lord!'

Out came a baby weighing eleven pounds, handsome as a Greek bronze, with features that looked as if they'd been finished off with a fine-tipped brush. In defiance of the Abacrasta gossips they called him Solicheddu, or little sun.

When he celebrated his seventh birthday, Mama Serafina gave him a pair of gold scissors. With these he began to prune the silverberry tree in the courtyard every winter. To his playmates who still ask him, even today, what fruits grow on the magic tree at his house, Solicheddu replies with a laugh:

'Whichever ones I want.'

'Why is that, Solichè?'

'Because it's the tree of life!'

15

Zirolamu Listinchinu

Zirolamu Listinchinu was the first of his clan to go in for 'booklearning'. After centuries of wild berries, horsehair and quails hanging up to dry in the chimney, at long last a Listinchinu held a degree.

For that family of goatherds his graduation was a historical event never to be forgotten. They had framed the parchment testifying to his doctoral title, conferred by the University of Stàffari, in light wood worked with dark mahogany, with floral ornamentation that made it look like a coffin. So that everyone could see it easily, they hung it at head-height in the sitting room, between a Sacred Heart painted in red ink with blood dripping from a wound and a picture of the Miraculous Translation of the Holy House of Loreto.

To the disappointment of his parents and sisters, people

ignored Zirolamu Listinchinu's doctor's degree in medicine, and paused instead in wide-eyed admiration before that picture, which was an enlargement of a church pamphlet. The Holy House of Loreto flew above a sky of frothy clouds, held aloft by three angels. A little higher up, an ascending Madonna and Child listened in ecstasy to the music of other angels playing the lyre and the lute.

The aunts who made the puddings for the occasion pulled out all the stops, making three times the usual amount of everything: glazed biscuits, amaretti, meringues, honey and almond cakes the size of your fist, discs of candied orange peel the size of LP records. For a month the Listinchinu household was filled with the smell of marsala, toasted almonds and steaming coffee pots.

The people of Abacrasta lined up to offer their good wishes. They came in envious, delivered an exhausting tide of compliments, and left resentful, cursing the medic.

'Ha! A lot of fuss about nothing. Zirolamu may be brainy, but he's not the only doctor in the world.'

'It'll be a while before he's as good as Dr Gaghisi.'

'He's going to have to read a few books and peer up a few arseholes if he wants to show that he didn't get his degree in exchange for a bag of chick-pea fritters.'

'We're every bit as good as doctors anyway.'

'Bantine the mayor was an educated man, and look what happened to him! You're better off not thinking too much.'

In Abacrasta, whenever anyone managed to demonstrate their ability to do something requiring a bit of effort, they were sacrificed slowly on the altar of ill will. The favourite pastime of most of the inhabitants was to trim their neighbour's grass as soon as it grew higher than a few inches.

Poor Zirolamu knew nothing of this, so he decided to climb even higher, and specialised in psychiatry. His father, who had some vague idea of the meaning of the word, vigorously advised him against it:

'Are you really going to study mad people, Zirò?'

There was a general surgery a stone's throw away, in the village of Melagravida, where Zirolamu could have spent his life prescribing syrups and suppositories, and instead he wanted to lock himself away in a madhouse.

'With all the people we know, you'd barely have to lift a finger. Visits, prescriptions, tons of money, suckling pigs at Easter, kids at Christmas, cheese, sugar and coffee all year round. I'd quit while you're ahead, Zirò, because if our kind climb too high, they tend to get vertigo.'

Achille Listinchinu was as stubborn as his son, and his mother, Iolanda Cambosu, was even worse:

'You've done quite enough already, my boy! Stop there! Work and bring up a family. You don't want to spend your whole life studying, do you?'

Deep down, Zirolamu had already made up his mind. Even if they cut off his funding, Professor Sambeneddu,

116

the head of the University Hospital, had promised to see about getting him a grant.

The future mad-doctor, as they were starting to call him in Abacrasta, wanted more than anything to find the spring within the clockwork of his peasants' minds that carried people off so prematurely.

Zirolamu's parents gave in to pressure from his nine sisters, and he passed his specialist studies with flying colours to the approval of everyone.

He had been passionate about medicine since childhood. He spent whole days anaesthetising dogs and cats with brandy, before opening up their bellies with a scalpel to see what was inside. All his savings, and the money he got on church holidays, he spent on anatomy books. By the age of nine he knew by heart all the systems, organs and tissues of the human body. His favourite present was from an uncle who worked in a car factory on the mainland. One summer when his uncle came back for the holidays he brought the boy a microscope. Zirolamu wept with joy.

When he grew up a little and started hearing stories about those strange deaths, he opened up dogs' and cats' heads with an axe to study their brains. Sometimes he studied the brain as a whole, trying to understand what it was that ran along those little rivers of blood that spread like a spider's web through the squidgy mass. Other times he separated the hemispheres with a clean butcher's chop, then reduced them to thin slices which he put on

117

microscope plates to enlarge the claret stains and the snow-white pulp.

The other boys played ball in the school playground, learned to milk goats, to hold their wine and soothe their girlfriends' early ardours with a cooling kiss. He got high marks in his school reports, the kind that embarrass even the teachers. And it was the same at high school, always straight tens, nothing but tens, even in religion and general behaviour.

In the Listinchinu household, woe to anyone who touched a hair on the head of their young prodigy. They wouldn't even let him pick up a piece of straw from the floor. His sisters had got themselves into this habit, even though Zirolamu himself was neither presumptuous nor naïve. They beat egg-yolk with sugar for him, they prepared his veal consommé, they boned his fish, they peeled his fruit.

'Leave it, Zirò! Don't worry, Zirò! I'll do it, Zirò! Don't exhaust yourself, Zirò!'

Whenever anything good came into the family home, be it food, shoes or clothes, he was given first choice. Zirolamu received this affection and mollycoddling almost with embarrassment, because he wanted to show the world that he too knew how to peel a pear and tie his shoelaces. But he put up with it so as not to offend his sisters and because it meant he could devote himself completely to his studies.

118

On the day he left for the University of Stàffari, his family wept for him as if he had died, or was leaving for the front. The journey was a hundred and fifty kilometres, there and back. In a fast car, even without travelling at breakneck speed, you could get there in just over an hour.

At the end of that year Zirolamu became the trusted assistant of Professor Sambeneddu, the head of department, and when he suffered a terrible shock and went out of his mind, Zirolamu stepped up and took the man's job on the eleventh floor, in the department devoted to lunatics and depressives of every hue.

His kindly predecessor had had an awful experience one morning, when he was kidnapped by two schizophrenic patients destroyed in body and mind by the pain of life. One was a teacher who couldn't accept retirement, and who walked around naked, hurling stones and books at passers-by. The other was a thirty-year-old policeman, abandoned by his wife and two daughters, who had tried one night to strangle them in their sleep.

They weren't even the most difficult patients in the department. When they grew restive, they were more easily calmed with a pack of sticky sweets than a heavy dose of Valium. Sometimes a smile, a touch, was enough for them to be as meek as freshly nursed babies.

That morning was different. Fausto and Gabriele somehow got hold of a stanley knife, a paintbrush and a tin of black paint. They had kidnapped Professor Sambeneddu during visiting hours on the ward, covered him with paint and cut lots of question marks all over his body.

'Answer! Why won't you answer?' they asked him as they finished their task on the restraining bed to which they had fastened him.

Perhaps they were seeking an answer to their illness, an answer which wasn't in the books and which Professor Sambeneddu couldn't give them. They left him more dead than alive, covered with blood and shit. He was miraculously saved in the intensive care unit at the local hospital, with oxygen and transfusions.

As the police brought them to the criminal asylum, Fausto and Gabriele laughed as if nothing had happened, as if it was someone else's business, nothing to do with them. As they walked to the ambulance, Gabriele turned to one of the guards who was holding him tightly by the arm, and asked him, 'Excuse me, mate, but where's our squad car? We're patrolling the district of Santa Maria, aren't we?'

Professor Sambeneddu was scarred by this terrible incident for the rest of his life. Once he had been released from hospital, he took to drink and became afraid of everything, even flies. He applied for permission to bear arms, and bought a big gun. He walked around schools and barracks carrying it, loaded, threatening any teachers and policemen who bore any resemblance to Fausto or Gabriele. In the end his wife was forced to move him to the mainland, to a private mental home.

This episode also made a big impression on Zirolamu, even though he had made allowances for certain unforeseen events arising from his job, and his veins ran with blood that was colder than the director's, the blood of the Listinchinus, who had been goatherds and horse-trainers for centuries.

To make the journey between Stàffari and Abacrasta, Zirolamu bought himself a powerful car, the kind that made you imagine horses appearing from beneath the bonnet when you put your foot on the accelerator.

He had three houses, each lovelier than the last. The one at the Sologai marina was the finest, with five acres of orchard and a roof garden that would have made a king green with envy. He was what is called a success, known and appreciated halfway around the world, publishing in specialist medical journals and lecturing at conferences and ministerial consultancies. Few people knew the insane and their illnesses as he did.

At the age of forty, all he needed to crown his existence was a wife. Mama Iolanda, now weak and embittered, said to him every time he came back to Abacrasta:

'Just bear in mind that a man without a family is worthless – even if he becomes President of the Republic – and leaves nothing on this earth! Sort yourself out and find yourself a wife, for heaven's sake! For the love of God, don't let me die with that thought in my head!'

Zirolamu was a wonderful doctor, but he was an idiot

with women. He either tried too hard or didn't say a word. He knew nothing of the techniques of courtship, and despised diplomacy, half measures meant nothing to him; it had to be all or nothing. He had never really had a love affair. A few quickies with ambitious nurses, two flings with colleagues on night duty, the odd prostitute and that was that.

To keep his mother happy and resolve the problem once and for all, he played the internet card. He began frequenting a chat room, and came into contact with a woman from Bustellu, a seaside village in the old mining area of the island. For a year they kissed and caressed via computer, composing long letters of love that travelled on the hidden waves of electronic mail, and then suddenly there was nothing.

They were going to see each other and get married and then, all of a sudden, it all blew over with a mysterious puff of electronic smoke. He had no idea whether the woman of his dreams really existed, no idea if Venerina Pilarda was made of flesh and blood or just an invention of his computer's memory. The fact is that the whole business made Zirolamu Listinchinu ill.

He soon became so distressed that he neglected his personal hygiene, began to visit the worst kind of bar and mix with the dodgiest of characters. It became hard to tell him apart from his patients. His eyes were wild and he walked slowly, as if carrying a sack of cement on his back. He stammered when he spoke, and would start to cry over the slightest thing, and ask for understanding and forgiveness for nothing whatsoever. The failure of his love brought it home to him: he had become a doctor, but he had never become a man. He felt this very intensely, crying over it and wailing like a baby smacked by his father for no reason.

One Thursday in late December he wrote one last letter on his computer and addressed it to pilarda@tron.it. A few substantial words, as was his style.

'I've decided to end it all. If you don't come to San Pancrazio Station at eight o'clock on Friday, your conscience will have to bear the failure of our love and the premature interruption of my life. Ever yours, in this world and the next, Zirolamu.'

Venerina didn't come that night. Zirolamu tanked himself up on wine from the barrel and stuffed himself with pizza. The rain was washing the streets as if they were sheets in a washing machine.

Wandering dully around the alleyways of old Stàffari, Zirolamu met a stray cat and brought it home under his coat. He put it down on the kitchen table and rummaged through the drawers for a carving knife. He stumbled, and could barely hold in his vomit. The desire to smash open the animal's head was uncontrollable.

He found the knife and then started stroking the cat on the back. They gazed into one another's eyes for a long time. The creature, cold and hungry, stared at him hopefully. Then Zirolamu vomited his pizza and wine onto the table, fell flat on his face, and the cat started licking the vomit and his cold ears. As he was about to drown in his acidic bile, Zirolamu heard the Voice:

'Ajò! Get ready, for your time has come!'

The mad-doctor, his head burning like an electrical short circuit, looked at his filthy chest and unbuttoned his heavy velvet shirt. His heart was there, concealed by a sheet of pink skin and his soft ribs.

'One good blow and I'll split it in half!' thought Zirolamu.

The cat went on licking at the stuff on the table. Zirolamu raised the knife in the air, and at that precise moment the doorbell rang. The effect of his drunkenness evaporated in a yellow cloud that rose all the way to the lamp hanging from the ceiling.

'And who could it be at this hour? The madmen won't even leave me in peace at night! Cursed be the hour when I decided to understand them!'

When he went to open the door he found Redenta Tiria standing in front of him.

'Good evening! Is this a bad time? I've got a letter for you here from Venerina Pilarda.'

The woman handed over the crumpled envelope and left. Zirolamu opened it with the nail of his little finger and read it in a breath:

'My life, don't make such threats even as a joke. My

124

computer keeps crashing, it only works when it feels like it, it receives from time to time and never saves, just like some people. I'm asking this woman, who says she knows you and who happens to be passing through, to get in touch with you. I arrive in Stàffari on Sunday morning, and when I do I will never leave you again. A kiss on the mouth from your Pilardina.'

I read the banns for Zirolamu and Venerina a few years before my retirement. They had a register office wedding because she wasn't a believer. Now they come to Abacrasta every weekend. They have a little pair of twins, a boy and a girl. One is called Tirio and the other Redenta. If you don't believe this story, take a trip to Stàffari, they live on Via Prunischedda Cumpria, at number 103. The house is the one with the painted pink walls, and geraniums flowing from the containers along the balcony railing.

16

Benignu Motoretta

Ziropu Seghegliu was born to train oxen and make
children. To this very day no one knows how many animals
he broke in throughout the whole of the province of
Barbagia, but he did leave a good dozen children, after the
Voice had done for the rest. But if it hadn't been for
Redenta Tiria, the soul-stealers would have taken his son
Benignu Motoretta as well.

Benignu, Ziropu's son, was the elder of a pair of twins.
He had spent the nine months in Mama Gruchitta's
spherical belly with his brother Seppeddu who, even then,
was an unbearable thug. By his own free choice, Benignu
was the first to tumble into the heavy cloth prepared by
Tzia Ciccita. Not because he had more of a lust for life than
Seppeddu, although that much was clearly apparent,
but just to use his fists, feet and elbows to free himself

126

as quickly as possible from their forced acrobatic cohabitation. Seppeddu was born a few hours later, by which time the midwife had given him up for dead. 'This one won't make it, Signora Gruchì! I think I'll just give you a nice injection, we'll empty you out and sew you all up again, OK?'

Hereabouts, twin births are considered a curse, because they multiply the number of mouths to feed. If two lambs were born, one was sacrificed or given to a child, just as Candidu Vargia had given a lamb to me. With children, though, it was different. If you lacked the courage to drown one in the well, or wring its neck, then you kept them both, particularly if they were boys. Some of Abacrasta's witches were experts at sending premature babies to heaven. One of them, Tzia Alipinta, turned them into cherubs after their first whimpers, by pouring hot honey down their nostrils and holding them upside down for a few minutes. Two attempts to sneeze, like kittens with colds, and the game was over. They turned an alarming greyish-red colour. '*Sa morte durche*', 'sweet death' was the name given to this, as if death didn't always have the bitter taste of the oily berries of the mastic tree.

Each time he got his wife pregnant, Ziropu informed his family slightly in advance. Halfway through dinner, when everyone was leaning on the enamel basin, finishing off their lunch, he raised his hands aloft like a priest serving

127

Mass and announced: 'We've ordered a new baby! The Seghegliu family is growing. May God and these arms keep it healthy!' We've ordered it, we're buying it: he was also speaking in the name of Gruchitta, the poor thing, treating her like a mail-order catalogue. Benignu and Seppeddu, who were the oldest and always chewing on something or other, knew that he made the decisions about how and when his seed would bear fruit. Gruchitta, who bore his love like the weight of a cross, lent only her husk. After the first few pregnancies she had resigned herself to the role of farm manager; she opened her legs without enthusiasm, both to him and to the midwife. Fate had, out of pity and respect, helped her by giving her wide hips – which were now almost worn out – and swelling her breasts like two clouds of colostrum. I remember her as an old woman when I was a child, with her pennyroyal-green eyes, liquid and sad, resigned to the burden of that ox-trainer, a man of carts and inns and bed and not much love. At the age of twenty, when she gave birth to her fifth child, she lost all her teeth. From then until her death, she had never stopped sucking coffee beans roasted on the top of the oven. God knows what pleasure she found in that bitter stuff that stained her tongue and lips.

She ate like a lost soul. Early in the morning after her sixth childbirth, she made a pile of wet sheets of *pane carasau* and poured some fried eggs with tomatoes and onions over them. She ate noisily, chewing slow and long with her whetted gums, without much appetite, as if even feeding herself was a duty. Then, all of a sudden, clicking her tongue against her palate, she gave herself over to groans of pleasure that she never uttered in bed. In the winter, the season of mandarin orange, she walked around the trees in the courtyard and didn't leave a single one at head height. She spread out her skirt and sat down on a stone to peel them, leaving a carpet of skins on the ground. She opened the fruits with her nails and took out the segments one by one, before pressing them into her mouth and spitting out the seeds.

By the time Benignu turned fifteen, there was no more need for Babbu* Ziropu to announce the arrival of another heir. He had worked it out all by himself, because in the next room, separated from the children's room only by a thin layer of unbaked clay and cat-scratched bricks, his father went to sleep with a series of groans on some nights, both short and long, that sounded like the plaints of a weary donkey, or mournful death-rattles. *Huumrrr, huumrrr*: he ground his teeth and snorted through his nose. That was the noise he made when he came.

While all the brothers were still alive, the house of Seghegliu was like a prickly pear tree, heavy with its spiny fruits ranging in colour from orange to purple. They had two main rooms as well as another one under the stairs, and there was a dunghill behind a grille in the corner that

Babbu: father.

collected the contents of the stable drains. There were days when their courtyard also provided hospitality for four or five pairs of oxen. Their owners brought them there yoked and sick with scurvy, poking each other with their horns and hooves and mooing from dawn till dusk. The dung was raked for the vines and the vegetable plot and a stomach-churning smell of digested hay clung to the clothes and hair. Babbu Ziropu wanted the dung damp and well macerated, because he maintained that it was more nutritious that way and the wine would be stronger. All his children were boys and out of principle he had decided not to send them to school. He was convinced that school filled your head up with nonsense, that it made you unfit for life and work. 'Teachers are people with time on their hands, they're ticks, parasites, failures who don't know how to make their living with their hands. They're worse than priests and politicians!' He never tired of telling his children that true culture was the culture of the fields and the pine forest, and to communicate with your neighbour, dialect was better than any dictionary. 'Too much knowledge only brings madness! What's anyone supposed to do with geography, geometry, all those numbers learned by rote? And then there's history, always the same: the rich always rich, the poor always poor! For taming oxen I've only ever used my hands!'

Benignu, meditating on certain of his father's sayings, sometimes locked himself away in the stable with the animals, and brought the oil lamp to keep him company. It was there one night that the Voice called him: 'Ajò! Get ready, for your time has come!' The voice was loud and imperious, just like his father's, which made him get a move on, fearing worse to come. When the Voice saw that the boy was still sitting watching the shadows that swirled in the sheet-metal ceiling, it became impatient and called him again, this time in dialect: '*Ajò! Irbrìgadi, ca su tempus tuo est'arribau!*' Benignu, to keep from hearing, blocked his ears with cow dung and fell asleep. If you ask him now, he will tell you that on certain issues his father's plain-speaking philosophy may be more valuable than the thoughts in the encyclopaedias that furnish the sitting-rooms of the houses of Abacrasta.

Benignu told me stories that I have never found in novels. Like the one about the dancer and the singers who arrived in the village one day for the feast of its patron saint. The wandering players came from Baralei, with a mobile stage pulled by an old lorry, two estate cars for the band, a sidecar for the owner and the star of the show: Gigina the dancer. They turned up in the Piazzi di Sa Udditta, amongst stalls of toys and torrone. *Pampapaaa, pampamparaaa*. Wind instruments, drums, guitars and an organ. All kinds of delights! Divine music and sweaty loins gyrating in colourful, glittering clothes. Gigina the dancer leapt like one possessed, and rubbed a rope between her thighs. Benignu and Seppeddu had crept off to see them in secret, bored of the usual Abacrasta faces, the old songs, the old games and far too much work. When their father found out he whipped them soundly for a month, thrashing them with his belt on alternate days. 'To keep the wound from scabbing!' he said. In line with his rustic pedagogical system, he wanted to show his firstborn that living like that, braying and kicking your heels, was the sort of thing that only animals were good at. 'Mules can sing and jump, too! Only whores show off their tits and God knows what all else and don't you ever forget it!' When they got back home, however, the two brothers had found him so well informed about the event that they suspected him of having been in the audience as well.

But that was how Ziropu Seghegliu was, take it or leave it, he knew no middle way. His time spent in jail and even bereavement hadn't changed him, and they wouldn't change his sons, with all their grievances, or their desire to sniff the arse of the world with a nose different from his. He was used to burying his emotions in the depths of his soul. When he felt an intense feeling about to pounce on him, he hid it under the stones. If the situation demanded, he showed his emotions in a shameless, violent way, as when a rag collector passed through Loghelis, giving out bottles of perfume and inflatable balloons in exchange for old belongings. In return for a bottle of lily-of-the-valley perfume and a handful of balloons, Gruchitta brought him in and gave him a bag of dilapidated sweaters and worn-out

132

shoes. She should never have done it! Ziropu unleashed all his jealousy in vile words and also raised his hands to her. 'I'll throw the axe at you if you bring men into the house again!' When he discovered that Gruchitta had also given him a coffee pot, from the plate-rack lined with cut-out paper from the shop, he picked up the cups one by one and smashed them against the gritty floor. The balloons, too, met a sorry fate. He poured the perfume down the stable grille, cursing the while: 'Sooner pig-piss than this filth!' For some time the smell of lily-of-the-valley mixed with the acrid smell of piss and dung.

Since the accident, I have been to see Benignu every Sunday at the House of Invalids. Even today, as soon as I reach the square, I find him with his face stuck to the window looking out over the valley. When I go into his room he greets me with a smile and always says the same thing: 'You know that even today I think I can still smell that mixture of shit and violets?' He tells me the story of his life till lunchtime, and when he speaks of Redenta Tiria his eyes fill with joy and he tries to get out of his wheelchair to walk, gritting his teeth and showing the swollen muscles in his arms. When he's forced to slam his backside back on the embroidered cushion, he exclaims with a gesture of ancient resignation: 'That's asking too much. The important thing is that I'm alive. Isn't that right, Battì?' You will read the events leading up to his accident in what follows: see if you believe it or not. He has told me a few things in

133

instalments, I have merely stitched them together, and out of the respect that I owe him, I'll let him tell the story.

Day and night, our house in the neighbourhood of Sos Tres Bundos was like an anthill. Animals and people constantly bumping into one another, exchanging mysterious glances of intent and compassion over a fate that had brought them together in that enclosure of crumbling stone and oak boards tied together with wire. The neighbourhood of Sos Tres Bundos was so called because, almost a century previously, three servant shepherds were born, sons of a father who wouldn't let them come back from the sheep-pen even to take communion on obligation days. When they grew up, weary of the whip and their every mouthful of bread being begrudged them by their father, they made common cause and slaughtered him, and gave him to the crows to eat. With the help of some fellow shepherds, they managed to escape justice and fled to the mainland. At the headland of S'Ungia 'e Crapa, or the Goat's Hoof, where they had their sheepfold and where they impaled and disembowelled their father, it is said that before they crossed the water, they left three devilish masks carved into the wood of the wild pear tree: three demon faces. Since then, the neighbourhood had been called Sos Tres Bundos, or the Three Demons, because if they hadn't been kin to the evil one, they would never have mutilated their father like that, tyrant or not, but simply killed him.

134

Plainly, being born in such a neighbourhood does not bring good fortune. For me at least that's how it was, and for most of my brothers too. My life and that of the whole family of Ziropu Seghegliu altered with the arrival of a convoy of motorcyclists who had met up in Noroddile for a province-wide gathering. Babbu Ziropu nearly screamed when he saw those throbbing monsters speeding along, leaning into the bends till they trimmed the grass in the ditch. The motorcycles slipped in front of his cart like stray meteorites. He started whipping his cattle till they bled, but felt as if he was frozen at the edge of the half-paved road. Dust for the cattle, tar for the bikes. He was deafened by the *brouuuuum brouuuuum* that emerged from their gleaming exhaust pipes, tapered like women's thighs, and a bomb exploded in his heart. Only once before had he experienced such a weird shiver, accompanied by a release of intermittent emotions, as powerful as an electric shock, and that was when he met Mama Gruchitta on the way back from the stubble field. He had taken her there and then, among the rock-rose seeds that got tangled in their hair, and that smell of grain that permeated her skin all the way to her belly.

From then on, that music that smelled of petrol and red hot pistons accompanied him as he worked and dreamed. He no longer drove his ox, but held on to imaginary handlebars and, spluttering, imitated the noise of the motorbikes. *Brouuuuum brouuuuum!* His eyes, gleaming like headlights, flashed with anguished sadness at not being able to ride and tame one of those metal monsters, his dog-like nostrils dilated in search of that perfume of lives lived to the full. My brother Seppeddu and I happened upon him talking to himself. 'They really go, those steel beasts! Even the cows want them!' For him, bikes became an obsession from which he couldn't free himself, because in spite of his limits, the man was aware that he would have neither the time nor the ability to tame one of those spoke-wheeled monsters.

From that day onwards, however, he became as meek and compliant as one of the oxen that had passed through his hands for training. He treated Mama Gruchitta gently, and some days he would come home with a jar of blackberries or a bunch of wild lilies. She nearly went mad. He suddenly became handsome in a way she had never known. Her eyes shone like pebbles in a river-bed, and she even regained the toothless smile of her babyhood. On their wedding anniversary, Babbu Ziropu came home with a radio that looked like a wardrobe. He had bought it second hand from an electrician. So as not to drop it in the street, he tied it to the front of his cart, among a few bales of hay. Goods for goods, words and music in return for two sacks of grain and a transport of stones. The electrician had also added two piles of records, round and grooved like sheets of *pane carasau* carved with a fingernail. Music entered our rooms and our lives like a kind of intoxication,

136

the sort of drunkenness that grabs you by the hair and doesn't let you sober up even if you throw yourself in a vat of icy water. In the end we were all singing, a band rehearsal without conductor, each one of us inventing an instrument to join in with the tunes that spilled from the loudspeaker's gilded weave.

Every now and again Babbu Ziropu improvised refrains of famous songs in his tenor voice. He seemed at first to have forgotten his love of motorbikes. But he hadn't, because shortly afterwards he gathered us all together in the courtyard to tell us of the great event. The rain was pelting down outside, as if God was furious, and we crouched like mushrooms under the green canvas umbrellas. We were already missing our younger brothers Antine and Lilliu, who had been carried off by malaria the year the mosquitoes grew the size of pigeons. Within just a few days they had swollen up in an anaemic delirium that took them straight to the cemetery, to the row where the innocent children were laid to rest. Babbu Ziropu's shirt was drenched, his velvet trousers almost sliding from his thighs under the weight of the water, dripping a halo of elongated droplets from his beret. Below his raw leather belt, buckled with a copper coin bearing the image of a bull's head, we could see a pair of off-white underpants. He wasn't carrying an umbrella, and he was proud never to have used one in his life. He thought they were for women.

137

He rubbed his bristly beard with the back of his hand and started talking in a loud voice to drown out the sound of the rain, which was turning into hail and clattering down on the floorboards of the stable like drops of cold lead soup. As always, he kept things brief and got straight to the point. 'I've made a decision.' That was what he said, before training his eyes on me like the barrels of a gun. At first I was scared, because I thought that in order to punish me for some misdeed or other he was going to make me a servant shepherd for Tziu Cirranca, who was even worse than the father of the Three Demons, and whose maids were only allowed home once a year, when he decided. His servants all turned into animals: you grew horns and a tail, forgot how to use words and ended up talking to the oak trees or falling in love with a hen. One boy who worked as a shepherd for him now occupies a room on my floor: he's completely insane, at night he barks like a dog and by day he bleats like a billy-goat. You'd be better off spending your whole life in the army than working with someone like Tziu Cirranca.

Something flashed along the yard wall of the farmyard before slipping into Tzia Lentosa's dovecote. The doves flapped up in panic and Babbu Ziropu began talking again. We all held our breath with fear. 'I've decided that we're going to buy a motorbike! We'll buy it even if it has to come down in pieces from the sky. Cost what it may, I repeat, we're buying it!' He said it quickly, with the smile

138

of a running centaur, challenging both death and the rain. 'We've saved the money, because it's been a good year, and there are more and more animals in need of training. We'll buy it new,' he went on, 'and it will be driven by Benignu, who is the biggest of you. He already knows how to ride a horse and doesn't have to do military service.' What he meant by these remarks, I've never understood. I just know that Seppeddu darted me a murderous glance through the pin-sharp curtain of hail. My father had already been in jail twice, the first time over some hamstrung cattle, the second over a stabbing during a game of *morra*. With a motorbike in the farmyard he'd have ended up back in there, I'm sure of it.

Ever since he'd seen them speeding along the road to Noroddile, the desire to cast aside the whip and grab a pair of handlebars had become stronger than he was. He could already see himself crouching low in the saddle, his nose on the speedometer and his nervous, tapering calves encased in long, slender boots. He could already feel his callused hands clutching the handlebars like holm-oak roots. When he tired of goading the cattle, he took them by the horns and stared them straight in the eye, as though hypnotising them, to make them understand that they had to obey him at all costs. 'You give in, or I'll crush you!' he would yell at them. He treated us children much the same, except he grabbed us by the ears. On the evening of the announcement in the courtyard he talked to me as if I too

139

were one of his oxen, giving me to understand that there was no way out: whether I liked it or not, I was to learn to ride the motorbike.

I did my practical training with Birilleddu, who drove the bin lorry for a living, but lived for his one true passion: motorbikes. He had a Lodola 250, with a souped-up engine and widely splayed exhausts. On Sunday evenings, when he would ride around the bends at Parasatta and along the straight at Su Ponte, he sped off like a bullet from a gun, brushing past the girls' legs in a rising scale of gear changes, stretching the accelerator cord to snapping-point. At my brother Costanzu's christening my father made him a godfather so that he would always have him at his disposal for help and advice. Now I hardly ever went to the fields with the ox-cart, waiting instead for the big event fixed for the end of the spring, when I would finally have my licence. I was submitted for the test by the pharmacist, in return for a suckling pig and thirty litres of good wine. Apart from my excitement, which I quelled in advance by breakfasting on two sheets of *pane carasau*, some quail and a few shots of grappa, the test went extremely well. I might have passed it even without a reference from the pharmacist, who was a hunting companion of the examiner.

The piece of paper they gave me while I waited for the official licence to be sent by the prefecture meant I could already start riding along the streets on my own, although without a passenger. As I waited for my own motorcycle to arrive, Birilleddu lent me an old 175 cc Stornello with the handlebars lowered to the level of the front rubber fork gaiters. He had put on a domed headlight and decorated the saddle with studded red leather and a little sheet metal fairing. It was the bike he'd had as a youngster and, so that it wouldn't pass unnoticed, he'd painted it yellow with lead paint that was practically phosphorescent. I'd made myself some knee pads with two cork ladles, tied on with strips of inner tube. Initially I also slipped a layer of cork under my back, to avoid being skinned alive on the tarmac. With that first bike I learned to bend and do wheelies, to caress the velvet blacktop and listen to the whine of the engine filling the air like bagpipe music. After a few weeks I could drive the Stornello along the road that led from Abacrasta to our vines in Sas Monzittas with my eyes closed.

My father got the bike for a straight half million. He paid an extra thirty thousand lire for the colour, choosing one in purplish-red to highlight the chrome tank trims and the trademark wings. This model, which he had first seen in a catalogue, and then for real in a showroom in Noroddile, was a Scrambler 450, with wide handlebars and a chrome dash. It arrived on the first of June at Talisèri railway station. From there we brought it home on the cart, garlanded like the Madonna of S'Urbale and sprinkled with some holy water that an aunt of mine, a nun, had brought back from Jerusalem. The blessing, which featured lots of sprinkled water and altar boys, was performed by Don Ilariu who also, at the end of the ceremony, tied a little roll of palm leaves to the handlebars as a good-luck charm. It was my father who thought of giving it a name: 'We'll call it Thighinisa, the Spark!'

With the ceremony over, I wheeled the bike into the street to mount it for the first time. I touched the decompression lever with my thumb and, after two false kicks, got the engine running. As it warmed up like a bread oven, all the onlookers enjoyed the spectacle, feeling the ground tremble faintly beneath their feet. The staccato thump of that big piston pumped inside the cylinder, a red-hot womb spewing forth noise and intoxication. My thighs gripped the soft saddle, warm as *sanguinaccio*, I took hold of the ox-horn handlebars and leapt on. *Brouuuuum brouuuuum!* the engine sang powerfully. There was tumultuous applause and a few tears were shed. Some people even threw handfuls of fresh grain, dahlia buds and confetti to celebrate this anomalous marriage between slowness and speed, fodder and gasoline, ox and engine. Rujola Priozza broke a plate on the ground to bring good luck and ward off misfortune.

Only Mama Gruchitta was nowhere to be seen. She was off on her own, weeping, but not with joy. She wept because as much as she feared fever she feared the tricks that cruel fate plays on us poor humans. She had never heard the Voice, but she knew that fate lurked around every corner, drunk and cross-eyed, furious and stinking, ready to trip up all those who, by ignoring the Voice, end up making an enemy.

Proud and upright as a Nuragic bronze, I made for the hairpin bends of Sas Concheddas. There, like a bridegroom of antiquity, I grew drunk on the wind. I barely touched the accelerator, and the bike responded by quivering its stout flanks and changing the sound that issued from its chrome mouth, from tender to furious. It climbed resolutely, agile as a mountain goat. On a stretch of straight road I took fourth gear to its limit and, past four thousand revs, I changed up to fifth and flew thundering towards the orgasm borne down to me on the mountain breeze from the peaks of Sos Thilingrones.

Brouuuuum brouuuuum! It was a pleasure that came and went, intermittently broken by the power of the brakes, ferrying emotions from my arse to my heart. I drove homewards on the dirt track, sending handfuls of black soil flying far beyond the ditches each time I accelerated. When I got back, my father looked at me as if I was some kind of divinity. His eyes were wet with a mysterious joy, even more so than the day when he had fathered me.

'You're the best, Benì! From this day forward, you will devote yourself to this roaring creature as you would to a little brother! Do you know what I mean, Benì? And mark my words, eh?'

143

A few years later, which I spent riding like a madman, I noticed I had grown up without love, and without hope. I lived with the bike and by the bike, I talked about nothing but carburettors, fuel supplies, forks, cylinders, dashes and pistons. I had lost my friends, and forgotten my work in the fields and become a professional thief, of the kind who creep up on animals even when they don't actually want to steal them. I also started drinking immoderately, convinced, like many peasants, that this was a solution to life's problems. Basically I was just one of those people who kill themselves a little bit every day, a slow and stupid suicide.

Babbu Ziropu, once he was through his motorbike craze, had resumed his role as a tyrannical father. He never missed a chance to curse the hour when he had decided to bring this monster into the house. 'A fine thing I've done!' My brothers didn't hold me in great esteem either, treating me like a hibernating snake. The people from the neighbourhood of Sos Tres Bundos went around calling me a hopeless case, a thief who left nothing in his wake, a weak-willed crook. Women of my age and younger called me 'the guy with the red bike', and held me at arm's length as if I had the plague. I satisfied my baser needs at the house of Ghelesia, a woman from Caràmas who accepted presents in kind and promises of marriage. Once I even brought her a live cow.

Then I started waking up every night, terrified of ending

my days alone like a mangy dog. I'd got myself into a fine state! I often thought, too, of killing my father, to make him pay for the idea of bringing me into the world and making me the person I was. When I came home drunk at one in the morning, he would yell at me, reminding me where I was headed. The desire to crack his head open with the axe would grip me and leave me exhausted. Morning and evening, the same litany: 'Look at the state of you! Aren't you ashamed of yourself? You're nothing but a murderer, can't you see that you're killing your mother before her time?' It was he who had brought me to this state, ordering me around like a general since I'd barely learned to walk. Go here, go there! Do this and do that! Some bloody childhood!

He had aged my mother before her time, impregnating her every year like a sheep. And he had the nerve to complain. He was the one who had chosen to deny us an education, to keep us far from the world, always at his disposal like beasts in a pen, to be milked with blackmail, flattery, threats. It was he who wanted to erect a barrier against the evils of progress all on his own and then, like some barbarian Odysseus, destroyed it, as soon as he heard the siren roar of those motorbikes racing towards Noroddile. Our family and everything to do with it had always depended on his moods, which he either masked or displayed like trophies. Whenever he noticed that a bit of freedom had come into the house along with the motorbike, throwing everything into confusion and threatening to topple him from his terracotta throne, he revealed himself in all his violent arrogance. He used his fists rather than his tongue wherever he could, and he walked all over Mama Gruchitta. 'It's all your fault, you've always been soft with your sons!' He reproached her at lunch and dinner, as if she was the one who had wanted the motorbike, as though bringing me into the world had been a mistake. My mother lived on remorse and tears. You wouldn't have wished such a life on anyone.

One evening when she saw us going head to head, spitting and fuming at one another, she announced that if things went on like that she would end up throwing herself in the well, she would follow the Voice. 'Better dead than living like this!' I loved her too much to let her take that course. For her I would have given up the wine, the bike, the thieving and the bad company. But what would have been the point? So I decided to excise the problem, since I myself was the blight of the family.

One afternoon when I had drunk more than usual I climbed on to the bike, and, wrenching it up to full throttle, climbed to the highest point of Sos Thilingrones. From up there I looked at Baràlai for the last time, eyes veiled with fury and teeth clenched in a grimace of rancour. The brown rooftops flaunted themselves in the sun, sending the music of slumbering silence up to the mountaintops. A few kestrels had abandoned their shady

146

nests in the limestone peaks, and now swooped like acrobats in the clear sky. It was at that moment that I heard the Voice again. This time it wasn't rough and malicious as it had been before, but affectionate, like the voice of a mother singing you to sleep: 'Ajò! Ajò, Benì, follow me, your time really has come now!'

Inside me I felt the fear of dying mingle with the fear of living. In the end my desire to spite the world, and my father, won out. Kickstarting the bike, I got it moving and jumped on. The slithering descent felt like a dark, oily snake. The zooming parapets that lined the bends were spurs that gave wings to my steel engine. Faces appeared at the edges of the ditch, people leaned forward to speed me on. I heard the applause, the voices. 'Come on! Come on, Benì, you're the first, the best!' The air was filled with the scent of tar, of dry hay, of speed and hot metal. Just before the wall surrounding the Scolovè fountain I shut my eyes and raised my feet and arms to meet my death.

The bike flew through the air for a moment, before blowing apart on the sculpted stones in a rosary of screws and bolts, leaving scraps of rubber and a trail of petrol strewn all over the road. I opened my eyes in a field of asphodels, convinced I was already in the afterworld, with all those white stems pointing towards the sun. The sky was dancing, just as it did when I was a child and pressed my eyelids with the tip of my index finger. Sketchy visions that quickly turned from orange to black, to pale green, to dark yellow. It was only when the first flies came that I realised that God the Father didn't want me, that my hour hadn't yet come. I wiped away the thick, icy sweat with both hands, and felt down to my knees to see if anything was broken. Nothing, not a scratch. Just a few scrapes on my elbows, and a shallow cut at the top of my right thigh.

Before I started calling for help, I tried to haul myself up. Christ alive! My back and legs wouldn't obey me, they'd left me of their own accord. *Shit, fuck, damn!* When I ran my hand across my back, around the height of my belt, I felt a strange crunching sensation and realised that I was lying on a comb of rock that stood out from the ground like a scab. So I decided not to shout, and just wait silently for death.

Redenta Tiria arrived before nightfall. She carried a bag full of rose petals over her shoulder, and without saying a word she scattered them around me. That night I was found by Boelle the roadman, who had dreamed of a barefoot woman telling him to go to the bend of the broken parapet of Scolovè and look down. 'Go and save a newborn child!' she commanded.

In hospital, even if not a living soul ever came to look for me, I was actually born for a second time. My father said I was dead and buried as far as the family were concerned. No one ever thought of straightening my broken spine. Too much money and too many risks, claimed all the specialists who came to see me. But I never

148

gave up, until I met Sister Giovanna, who could be Redenta Tiria's twin sister. She alone, like the strength the blind woman gave me, has never abandoned me. In my pain they have been my father, mother and Almighty God. To Redenta Tiria I owe my life, to Sister Giovanna my wheelchair, and my desire to go on listening to the icy wind that blows between the shutters of the windows that gaze out beyond the infinity of Abacrasta's House of Invalids.

17

Ciriacu Pistola

The court didn't even recognise any extenuating circumstances, and gave him a twenty-year sentence. He was thirty at the time; he would be fifty when he came out, with rather less hair and his teeth ground down by shame and indignation.

'Deliberate homicide aggravated by premeditation.'

Before the gowned judges withdrew, putting the case file away in a yellow folder, Ciriacu Pistola swore before them, and before God:

'I did not kill Dionigi Lamentu! You're sending an innocent man to jail!'

Four prison guards slipped handcuffs around his wrists and, passing through the underground corridors of the court, loaded him into the armoured police van parked in the courtyard. His destination was the prison at Albudera, an old medieval fortress converted into a jail for criminals who represented a severe danger to society. In the summer heat, throughout the whole of the journey, there was only one short cigarette break.

'Ten minutes!' said Brigadier Casu. 'If you need to drink or piss, hurry up, because you won't be doing either in the open air for another twenty years.'

He said it without malice, and even took the handcuffs off, because he understood criminals and Ciriacu Pistola, in spite of his nickname, Shotgun, didn't have the look of someone who would leap into the precipice, risking a burst of machine-gun fire.

Wrists stiff, and hands numb from clenching his fists with rage, Ciriacu tried to open his flies to urinate. He found himself shrunken to a tiny bud. To avoid pissing in his trousers, he arched his back and tried to force himself to go, squeezing his kidneys like sponges. He waited for a few minutes like that before giving up. Not a drop.

He was put back in the van with his wrists free. To avoid getting carsick as they proceeded along the tongue of tarmac that was swallowed up beneath the wheels, Ciriacu shut his eyes and started thinking.

He had been arrested six months earlier, a few hours after the crime, during his first milking of the day. Thirty policemen had turned up at the sheepfold, and told him to drop his weapons and put his hands up. He had obeyed, leaving a sheep half milked. It was from that moment that

151

his torment had begun, first stop the village of Badu 'e Canes, or Dogs' Ford. Discussions with trustworthy lawyers (his father had appointed two of the best in Noroddile), a cooped-up life, the television on all day, endless games of draughts and trumps, in which the only winner was the slowly passing time.

'You'll get off, you'll see!' his cell-mates told him. 'They haven't an ounce of proof against you, nothing but rumours and circumstantial evidence!'

The circumstantial evidence was a dirty shirt found at the home of the victim, Dionigi Lamentu, a glass with Ciriacu's fingerprints on it, and a handkerchief soaked in evaporated sweat. Many rumours circulated, beginning with the ones that said he was a lover of the victim's wife, Rimunda Carteri, and ending with the grazing disputes he had had with the victim. Dionigi and Ciriacu had on occasion confronted one another with knives and hurled insults at each other over the boundaries of their lands in Sos Pedicurzos and Sas Umbrosas, but things had always ended over a bottle of wine, without rancour.

That was the kind of men they were. When they hated each other they were capable of tearing each other's heads off for a foot of ground, for a badly made fence, for three sheep drinking from the wrong spring. When they were at peace, however, they swapped lunches and favours: they had served together in the military, and that service received the honours due to it.

They had competed over Rimunda Carteri for a few years, before Ciriacu had given up, having worked out that if he didn't they really would end up shooting each other. On the night of the murder, Ciriacu had helped Dionigi to unload a cartful of hay bales, and then they had gone back to his house for dinner.

Before starting out on the tractor they went, bare-chested, to refresh themselves at the water hole. They threw handfuls of water over each other, playing like children, at risk, as always, of the joke turning into a tragedy.

'*Agàbala!* Stop it, Dionì, or I'll wrestle you to the ground!'

'Try it, if you're man enough! Wasn't it enough the last time? You want some more? I'd think about finding another shirt instead of that ragged one you've taken off, because they're not going to want to carry you home in that state!'

As they had been unloading the bales, the end of a piece of wire had got caught in Ciriacu's shirt and torn it in two.

'And where am I going to find a decent shirt at this time of day? In the shops?'

'Don't fuss so, you fool! I'll lend you one of my work shirts. They're hanging up on the hooks on the door, next to the overalls and the milking trousers.'

Ciriacu rolled up his torn shirt and threw it on the ground, next to the feed sacks. He combed his hair with his hands and showed his white teeth to a rippled mirror that hung from the wall.

They climbed onto the tractor and set off back towards Abacrasta. It was the time of day when the sun drew long, unbroken shadows over the plain of S'Avenargiu. In the sky, beyond the peak of Urture, a white cloud floated slowly by, looking like some poor soul devoured by leprosy.

They parked in the big farmyard and uncoupled the cart from the tractor.

'It's got late! I was starting to get worried!' said Rimunda, coming down to greet them.

Dinner consisted of stewed lamb, roasted sausages, fresh cheese cooked on a hot stone and lots of red wine. The Lamentus' rustic kitchen was like a furnace. They poured their first glass, then Dionigi disappeared for a moment to check two sheep that he had left in isolation in a little stone enclosure. They had been hit by a car, and seemed to have had some sort of internal haemorrhage.

'Have you fed and watered them?'

'Yes, twice,' answered his wife.

When he came back from the farmyard, Dionigi looked resigned:

'They'll have to be slaughtered tomorrow morning. They're bleeding at the mouth and they haven't touched their feed.'

He took the bottle and refilled the glasses to the brim.

By the hearth, Ciriacu poked the fire and turned the sausages on the spit, every now and again dripping the fat onto some bread in a wicker basket. The warmth from the wine, along with the heat of the fire, gave him the appearance of Lucifer, even though he had the features of a Baby Jesus stolen from an icon.

He looked at Dionigi sitting opposite him and, when he had the chance, glanced over towards Rimunda, who was busying herself at the stove with pots and pans. Sweat poured down his forehead and his checked handkerchief looked like a wet ball. He set it down on the edge of the fireplace and let the sharp-scented sweat drip down his face, stinging his eyes.

'Taste it and see if it's salty enough, Cirì!' she said, coming over with a wooden spoon full of steaming sauce.

Ciriacu touched the sauce with the tip of his tongue and exclaimed, 'That's very good! It would bring the dead back to life! My compliments to the cook!'

Suddenly Rimunda was blushing and then, turning her back on him and returning to her task, she asked:

'Which would you rather have first, the lamb stew or the sausages?'

'What are you on about?' replied her husband. 'Let's take the sausages off the fire so they don't dry out, and eat them afterwards.'

They had their umpteenth glass of wine and then sat down at the table. By the time they got up, their legs trembling with all they had eaten and drunk, it was just past ten. Before he left, Ciriacu turned to Dionigi and said jokingly:

'That stringy cheese was just too good, my old mate! Is it really yours? I didn't know you could make cheese as good as that!'

'Be off with you,' the other man replied, 'I've got to go to the sheepfold now and separate those two lambs from the rest of the flock.'

'We'll see each other soon, and in good health! Goodnight, Rimù, once again my compliments and thanks for dinner.'

Those were the last words those two old mates-at-arms said to each other, because from that moment on they never saw each other again. To be precise, Dionigi never saw anyone again, because at midnight he was found, lying in the threshold of his front door, with his legs sticking out and the rest of him inside. He was still clutching the wine bottle, as if he had just raised a glass to his murderer. His face had been blown to pieces by a single gunshot, one blast from a rifle that had thrown him several yards.

Whoever had done it was someone who knew him, 'an insider', as the investigators soon said.

In court, the shirt, the glass, the handkerchief, the old arguments over boundary violations, the unrequited love of the dead man's wife, the suspect's passion for firearms, all in all brought him a twenty-year sentence. Ciriacu's father, Tziu Bachis Manteddu, followed the trial in silence, paid the lawyers, then went to look after the family herd with a servant shepherd he had taken on to replace his son. When sentence was passed he said not a word and shed not a tear. Only a shadow of sadness veiled his eyes for a moment, then he turned once more into the dour character he had always been, walking with his chest thrown out, with the proud expression of someone who can challenge the world without fear of anything.

He had been left a widower when Ciriacu was just six, to be both the boy's father and mother, and that in a village like Abacrasta, where sometimes the women are better at doing the work than the men. He himself had given his son the nickname Pistola, when he had taught him to shoot at tree trunks and tin cans. Ciriacu had the eye of a hawk, he could knock down a target from thirty paces without taking aim. In the army, his superiors watched him open-mouthed, because he could outshoot everyone in the whole battalion.

That openly declared passion, along with his other one, less plainly apparent but common knowledge nonetheless, turned circumstantial evidence into certain proof, and opened the doors of Albudero jail to him. Seen from without, the prison looked like something else, a museum, perhaps, or a town hall. Inside, on the other hand, it was frightening, a circular building that stretched out its

157

radiating arms towards the paved eye of the courtyard, the one where the inmates spent hours looking busy and doing nothing.

There is nothing to be said of Ciriacu's vicissitudes and behaviour during those years. We need only know that he never had a row with anyone, neither with the guards nor with his fellow prisoners, and that he spent much of his time reading the books he borrowed from the library.

Between those whitewashed walls, scratched with names, addresses, broken hearts, obscene words and drawings, the Voice had never been heard. And Ciriacu had been waiting for it for a long time, had been waiting to roll up his sheet and hang himself from the bars of his narrow window.

He had been imprisoned on a day when the smell of salt penetrated the skin and the sound of the sea reached the cells, wailing along with the hot *sirocco* wind. He came out aged with grief. Nothing outside had changed except the models of the cars and motorbikes, the uniform of the policeman who directed the traffic near the gate, the lights around the old fortress. The people by the seaside were just as he had left them twenty years before – shorts, brightly coloured shirts, sunglasses, tanned skin, with the quick gait of people who walked without knowing where they were going, the walk of those undecided between swimming and walking.

Tziu Bachis hadn't sent anyone to collect him. Ciriacu

asked the traffic policeman for information about bus departure times and, clutching his plastic bags filled with bad memories and personal effects, he made for the bus station. The first coach for Noroddile left late that afternoon. From there, unless the timetables had changed, he would have time to catch the last bus to Abacrasta.

The sun beat down hard, like a hammer. Ciriacu bought a pair of aviator-style sunglasses from an African street-trader and set them on his nose. Wearing them, he saw everything in cucumber green, the chairs outside next to the kiosks, the sky, an aeroplane taking off like a huge seagull.

He bought his ticket, sat down on a bench and looked at the world around him, to allow his senses to adjust to sounds, smells and colours once more. When a skinny man pedalled past him on his little ice-cream cart, he went over and ordered one.

'Fill me the biggest cone you've got,' he said.

The man looked at him strangely and then asked him almost with irritation:

'What flavour?'

'You choose,' replied Ciriacu.

'Lemon's a house speciality.'

'OK, then,' said Ciriacu.

He went and sat down. He licked his ice-cream slowly, almost as though counting the days he had lost in jail, buried without a cross between the four walls of a cell where some other poor soul was now rotting. Perhaps someone innocent, like himself.

By the time he reached Abacrasta it was already dark. The gas lamps that had formerly spewed their honeyed light across the streets were no longer there. In their place were tall lamp posts with white bulbs that looked like snowballs. His father welcomed him with a cold hug and a bottle of good wine that he had set to chill behind the well.

That evening they didn't say a word. They just looked at each other, sniffing at each other like dogs meeting up after being separated by misfortune.

'Good night, see you tomorrow,' they said to each other before they went to bed.

'Have a good rest, we have serious things to talk about tomorrow,' added Tziu Bachis.

'I've been resting for twenty years,' replied his son. 'I think I'll go out for a walk in the village.'

He showered in the new bathroom, put on clean clothes and went out. Abacrasta had changed in twenty years. New houses where old ones used to be, roll-up shutters, grilles over ground-floor windows, bars with neon signs, drunken teenagers playing *morra* in a field of beer cans, a public garden with a big, empty swimming pool, the façades of the churches painted up like old whores, two gaming arcades, four open-air pizza parlours, people walking up and down the street without knowing where they were really going, like the people in Albudero, except that in Albudero there was at least the sea to keep you company with its beautiful voice. The young people fiddled with mobile phones, sending messages to other young people who were only a hundred yards away.

No one recognised him with his moustache and dark glasses. Below Rimunda's house a young man was sitting in the open air sipping on a beer. He looked like someone who didn't socialise very much. When the headlights of a passing car lit up his face, he thought he was looking at a photograph of himself from his days in military service. The young man had Ciriacu's nose, his mouth, the same falcon's-wing shape to the eyebrows. He walked straight on, he would go and talk to the widow the next day, his mind full of memories. There wasn't a single star in the sky, just clouds rising like soap bubbles from the Alenu river.

He reached the peak of Sos Alinos, sat down on an old tree trunk and looked down at the village. The noise from the splayed exhaust pipes of the mopeds drowned out the sound of the cicadas.

He went to sleep up there until he was woken by the dewy damp penetrating his bones. At the spring near the abandoned mine, he plunged his head into the stone basin and left it there until he felt his lungs begin to burst. At the age of fifty, physically at least, he had come out of jail stronger than he had gone in.

He strode back to the village, thinking of the questions he had to ask Rimunda Carteri. He knocked three times on

161

the door, which was opened by the young man he had seen sitting outside the evening before.

'What sort of time is this to go waking people up? Can I help you?' the young man asked.

'Is Signora Rimunda there? I'd like to talk to her,' said Ciriacu.

'Mà! There's someone here to see you.'

Rimunda emerged from the darkness like an angel. She was still beautiful, and wore a long, light nightgown, turquoise with little white flowers on it. She rubbed her eyes, recognised him straight away and invited him into the kitchen, as though she had been waiting for him, as though no time had passed.

'Come in and I'll put on some coffee.'

The kitchen was exactly as he had left it that evening. The only new things were a big television, a stereo system, a computer and books scattered around all over the place.

'The young man who opened the door to you is my son Dionigi. He was born six months after you were arrested. The dear departed died without knowing he was expecting an heir.'

'I had no idea,' replied Ciriacu. 'In twenty years I haven't spoken to a soul. Only my father wrote me the occasional letter, to tell me about the good years and the bad, the price of milk and cheese, the weddings and the funerals. And that's all, it was as if I wasn't anyone's son.'

Rimunda brought in a tray with cups on it.

'How much sugar?'

'None! In jail I got used to drinking it without.'

Rimunda didn't pick up on what he said, left the room for a moment and came back with a little basket of biscuits. She calmly began dunking one in her coffee. Staring at the waxed tablecloth, she asked him:

'And what do you have to tell me?'

'Nothing in particular. Sentence served in full, except for signing on at the police station, part of my life fed to the pigs as if I was a slice of overripe melon.'

Rimunda couldn't summon the strength to look up.

'But you should have lots of things to tell me. I've had the courage to pay my first visit to the wife of the man I'm supposed to have killed, and I'd like to have a few questions answered.'

Rimunda dunked the rest of her biscuit in her coffee cup, and pushed back her hair. She didn't have a single grey hair, it was all still red and curly like the beard on an ear of maize.

'I'll ask them all at once, and then, if you want to, you can reply at your leisure, otherwise I'll turn on my heels and you'll never see me again.'

Rimunda coughed and looked up towards the first rays of light fluttering through the shutters of the window.

'And what might those questions be?'

Ciriacu fanned the fingers of his hand and pretended to count.

'Why, during the investigations, did you never say a word? Why didn't you come and give evidence at the trial? You knew I was innocent. And I'm sure you knew the name of Dionigi's murderer. Who was he? Who is he? Is he still alive?' Rimunda swallowed. Her face began to streak with tears.

'I swear I don't want to sully my conscience by killing anyone,' he went on. 'I have no intention of going back to jail. I just want to know so I understand. In those twenty years I have done nothing but try to give a face and a name to the scoundrel who put that cross on my back.'

Rimunda sighed and didn't reply. Ciriacu finished his coffee and made to get up.

'*Adiosu*, Rimù! We will never meet again! I hope you can go on living in peace with your filthy conscience!'

When Ciriacu was about to leave, Rimunda called to him:

'Wait, Cirì! Come back and sit down! Don't leave, because I carry within me a weight that I can share with you alone.'

In a liberating flow of tears, interrupted only by short pauses, she told him the whole truth. The young man who had opened the door to him was the son of Ciriacu's father, Bachis Manteddu. He had taken his love by force, that week when she had gone to have the injections to cure her of St Anthony's fire. She hadn't said a thing to anyone, and when her period hadn't come she had gone mad with

164

worry. After a visit to a specialist only three people knew that Dionigi couldn't give her children: she, the party in question and the doctor in Noroddile.

On the day of the murder, when they were in the fields unloading hay bales, Tziu Bachis had turned up at the house, threatening her and telling her either to lock herself away or have an abortion.

'If you even think of telling Dionigi, I'll kill both of you. Or all three of you, since there's that bastard in there!'

She said she would wait until the following day, then she would tell him and ask his forgiveness.

'I'll kill him this evening when he goes to check on the lambs. Take care, Rimunda, take care! Don't play with fire!'

After her husband's death, Rimunda brought her pregnancy to term wearing full mourning, and kept the child. She called him Dionigi to make the people of the village believe that he was her husband's son, but you could tell from half a mile away that he was a Manteddu, from the way he spoke, the way he walked, his features, a strange way he had of lifting his right shoulder whenever he met anyone. But people put two and two together and thought he was the son of Ciriacu, the old suitor who had never managed to forget her.

'The dear departed must have discovered everything. That was why Ciriacu Pistola shot him in the face point-blank without even taking aim.'

'This time it had nothing to do with pastures or boundary disputes, it was all about jealousy. Otherwise they'd have come to blows and made up again the way they did the other times.'

'Oh, he was a hot-head, that one. They say he wasn't even recognisable after that shotgun blast.'

That was what people said in Abacrasta.

Ciriacu said goodbye to Rimunda and, his heart in turmoil like the sky before a storm, he went home. There was no one there. His father was in the fields tending to the animals.

He threw himself into bed and tried to fall asleep. He couldn't. He stared at the ceiling, trying to project onto the white background visual images of all the things that had happened during that night. His father calling Dionigi's name, Dionigi opening the door having recognised the voice, the bottle of wine and the glass to invite him in as he did on other occasions, the flash of rifle-fire stripping his face to the bone, the sound of his body hitting the floor like a sack of oats. *Sdrummm!*

At that moment he heard the Voice calling him:

'Ajò! Get ready, for your time has come!'

He had no desire to go back to jail for patricide, it would have meant spending the rest of his days behind bars. Better off dead! He looked at the leather belt that the guards had returned to him after twenty years. It was still good and stout. He went out to the farmyard, and into the

166

old shithouse. The struts under the roof were a bit worm-eaten, but they would hold the weight of a human being.

He brought over a wooden stool, took off his belt and tied it around his neck. *Tap, tap, tap.* Someone was knocking at the door, which was made of sheet metal nailed to boards.

'Ciriacu? Open up, I know you're in there! I urgently need to speak to you!'

His face darkened with shame, Ciriacu put his belt back on and opened the door. Redenta Tiria moved her sightless eyes as though looking him up and down:

'Forgive me for disturbing you, but this morning I met an old man in the street who told me to tell you some important things.'

They went into the kitchen together. Redenta followed the sound of his footsteps but didn't sit down. She accepted only a glass of fresh water, before telling him the news she had for him:

'On the road out of the village I met an old man waiting for the bus. He came over to me to ask me a favour. A strange favour, to tell the truth, the kind that not many people would be willing to do. He introduced himself, he told me how to get to his house, and he began to speak: "For the love of God, go to my son Ciriacu and tell him that he will never see his father again, that he is to consider him dead. He, left without a mother as a child, deserved a better father, and I, on a whim, dishonoured him and left him without a father too. Tell him I have gone far away, that I have dragged my foul carcass off to die elsewhere. I have a horrible disease that is devouring me from within, and I don't want to die looking him in the eyes. I no longer have the strength or the courage. I have been silent for twenty years, like a coward, and I can't talk now. Tell him to think of my son, his brother, and tell him not to abandon and betray him as I have abandoned and betrayed my son. That boy doesn't even seem like a Manteddu. He's good, well-behaved and studious. Tell Ciriacu to help him get his degree and a good job. My savings are registered in the name of Ciriacu Manteddu. If he can, let him forgive me for the harm I have done to him, to Rimunda and to the dear departed Dionigi. Goodbye!" He had time to say all that. And then he got on the bus for Porto Cirros and his voice faded away.'

'And this man you met, what was he like?'

'I couldn't tell you exactly. I have been blind since birth, and I form my own particular images of the people I meet. He must have been tall and imposing, with a weary face, creased with wrinkles of curdled pain, topped by prematurely white hair. His voice seemed to come from a long way off. His skin gave off a smell of old velvet and every now and again he whistled with his tongue between his teeth, as though he was missing an incisor or two.'

What the blind woman had just given him was the portrait of his father. Ciriacu took his head in his hands and closed his eyes to hold back the tears. When he opened them again, the barefoot woman with the raven hair had disappeared. Perhaps she had never been there, perhaps he had dreamed it all, the belt, the Voice, the stool, their conversation.

He went to the bedroom and tried on the suit he had worn on the day of Rimunda and Dionigi's wedding. It still fitted him. Wearing that, and a red carnation that he had found on the kitchen table, he went to ask for the hand of his late friend's widow.

For anyone who is sceptical and doesn't believe in these stories, I should add that they are all still alive and happy. Dionigi graduated in agricultural studies, and is head of the farmers' association in Noroddile. Ciriacu is a big landowner, and on Sundays he and Rimunda take flowers to the cemetery and polish the bronze angel on the tomb of the dear departed, alongside the headstone bearing the inscription:

'Cruel hands tore him from life, work and family.'

In Abacrasta, where everything is a mystery that condenses into clouds of bitter smoke, no one says anything now. No one but Tzia Rubinia Scarpuzza, the madwoman, who talks to herself and says:

'It was written thus! It was really written thus from A to Zed!'

18

Lazzaru Perdisciu

Lazzaru Perdisciu was born in Chentu Canes, the smallest neighbourhood for miles around: not much work there, not much bread, not much joy.

In those twenty houses built of breeze-blocks and bits of rubble, the only thing ever to be found in abundance is children. No sooner have they learned to walk on their own than others are born, as though the inhabitants were in a hurry to pass on their sole legacy: poverty.

Chentu Canes is a stone's throw from Abacrasta, just below the limestone blades of Monte Ziloche. But the people of the village look upon the disinherited folk of Chentu Canes as dogs, and treat them worse than dogs. Just after the war, the neighbourhood was given that accursed name – One Hundred Dogs – by a priest called Loricas, because there were ten shacks and a hundred people, almost all of them unbaptised and coupling at random.

Since then, the neighbourhood of Chentu Canes has grown. There are twenty shanties now and two hundred people, as if respecting a sacred law of poverty. On the only paved road, which runs through the place like a grass snake, even today you will find disembowelled washing machines, car engines and bits of bodywork, television sets belly up in the sun, chickens, dogs, pigs and more cats than you could count. A naïve passer-by might immediately wonder what those animals eat. They live on leftovers, like the people who live there, and by their wits.

One day, in one of those houses, on a bare, broken-springed bed frame, Lazzaru Perdisciu was born. They called him Lazzaru, meaning a leper, because his legs were short and left half-paralysed by a difficult birth.

The only stroke of good luck in his life was the fact that his father had stolen a stereo and a box of records from the people at the carnival. Thirty yards of cable were connected up to the electric wires that ran above the houses, and on came the music. From that day, the neighbourhood of Chentu Canes was like a funfair. Songs at all times of day or night, from radio stations and records on the turntable. While the bigger children were trying to find something to live on, Lazzaru was fiddling with knobs and valves. It was his salvation, in every sense. Listening to the music of the English and American bands, he started

171

singing and dancing on his own, as if he had been bitten by a tarantula. The twist, rock and roll and rhythm and blues, all at full pelt. His legs and his chest began to grow until there was no stopping them.

His father Perilao was flabbergasted.

'What on earth are you doing, watering him, to make him grow like that?' he asked his wife. She always replied with a gap-toothed smile.

'He's got it all from me! He's going to be a famous singer, mark my words. Can't you see how he moves? Can't you hear his voice? He's like a nightingale!'

In 1965, Lazzaru was six years old. His father took him to Noroddile for the first time, on the back of an old motorbike that only moved at all by blind faith. In the late afternoon, in Piazza Arborea, a music promoter was introducing singers and bands from the island, and selecting new artists to launch. The van publicising the event had driven round all the surrounding villages.

'Do you have a great voice? A good look? Can you dance? Artists from the whole of Barbagia, get ready, because your moment has come! At 6.30 this evening, in Piazza Arborea in Noroddile, don't miss the chance of a lifetime! 6.30, I repeat! Free entrance.'

Signor Gesualdo Paglia was the name of the man in charge of this kind of musical travelling circus. He was obese with a mop of fair hair, slicked back and clumsily brushed to the right-hand side.

172

When Lazzaru's turn came, his father paid ten thousand lire to a fat secretary, and his parents were showed to some chairs in an old gymnasium. The judge of the show, a bigwig with effeminate movements and fake eyelashes, led the child onto a stage, gave him the microphone and put on some music. It was a record by Chubby Checker: 'Let's twist again! Come on everybody . . .'

Lazzaru started singing with a black man's voice, twisting around on his legs, gyrating his pelvis, and waving his arms like an epileptic. At the end of his display he was dismissed with a few polite words:

'The kid has talent to burn. Perhaps one day he'll be someone, but at the moment, he isn't the one we need for our shows. Good luck.'

To get hold of the ten thousand lire, Perilao and his wife had collected money from everyone in Chentu Canes. Unwilling to return to Abacrasta empty-handed, father and son took a stroll backstage, where the artists were practising their numbers. They found themselves among walls of amplifiers, pedals, buttons, lights, batteries, saxophones and microphone stands.

'One, two, three . . . testing, testing . . .'

Perched on a wooden chair, the folding kind that you find on the beach, a foreigner, his blond hair in a pony-tail, was practising on his electric guitar, which was unplugged, and singing over it a song by Cream, *Sunshine Of Your Love*. The rhythm of the chords was dry and obsessive, like the

173

tune for a village dance played by a drunk. *Da-da-da dum, dum dum dum da-daa-dum.* Lazzaru watched and listened in ecstasy. At that moment a sound technician arrived and called the artist onto the stage:

'Ajò, Peter! Would you come and check this bloody Marshall amp, a valve must have blown!'

The fair-haired man left his guitar on the chair and, from behind the wings, leapt onto the stage. Quick as a hawk, Perilao grabbed the guitar and disappeared through the crowd with his son, making for the car park where he had left the motorbike. The old two-wheeler flew and in twenty minutes they were home. They found a second-hand amp for the Gibson, a Meazzi that had been painted ruby red.

With that guitar, Lazzaru grew up as a person and as a musician. He never learned a scale, he never read a note or a score, and he played and sang by ear, singing like a god and playing even better.

He first performed at village fêtes at the age of thirteen, as a guest on other people's stages. Next came his solo gigs, and then his own band – two guys from Noroddile, one on rhythm guitar and the other on drums, and a girl from Ispinarva on bass, Brigitta Bruscheris, so called in honour of Bardot.

He made swift progress, always stressing his humble origins:

'The cursed man of island rock! The six-string bandit!

174

The guitar genius of Abacrasta!' the headlines raved.

The group was originally called Sos Poverilos – The Poor Boys – and then, as things turned out, when the million-lire contracts with the record companies came in, and that name became meaningless, they changed it to Chentu Canes, like the neighbourhood, because although there were only four dogs on stage, they made enough noise for a hundred.

After a period playing covers of foreign songs, they started up their own repertoire in the local language, mixing genres that had absolutely nothing to do with one another. When one old bagpipe player plucked up the courage to speak of 'prostitution' rather than 'contamination', referring to their manner of stripping their ancestors' music of its roots, he was taken for a madman, and no one listened to him. Rather than diminishing, their success increased. The honeyed mixture of ethnic music stirred up with rock and blues drew fans to their concerts like wasps to tree-sap.

Mainland music critics hurled around grandiloquent superlatives as they attempted to define a kind of music that eluded definition, to find origins for these sounds which were merely the product of the neighbourhood of Chentu Canes, of poverty as black as Lazzaru's voice.

No one ever discovered the truth about Lazzaru Perdisciu's existential despair, because he kept it hidden away beneath his skin, like a disgrace, a mortal sin. Lazzaru had forgotten about his parents and brothers in Abacrasta. Every now and then he sent money and greetings, came home and then disappeared again on enormous aeroplanes, like a meteor. The people of the village, who were not given to vanity, and not keen on birds that flew too far from the cage, dismissed these events with a few sharp words:

'Lazzaru Perdisciu? Mad he was and mad he'll stay!'

'He'll soon end up on his arse. The Perdisciu family has never had to cope with that sort of money.'

'He'll end up like the flock of sheep that wandered a field of medicinal herbs, he'll die of too much success!'

If these observations were not ill omens, they were remarkably accurate predictions of what was to come.

Lazzaru toured the world. Cars, private planes, women – when he left one he found a hundred more. But the Voice followed him to every corner of the world, waiting for the right moment to whisper something in his ear. It was one evening when they were playing in Munich. There were thirty thousand paying spectators, advertising banners singing his and the group's praises and ovations before they even got on stage.

'Kentu Kanes! Kentu Kanes!' cried a great crowd of young people already out of their minds on beer, dope and amphetamines.

When the four stepped out on stage, Lazzaru didn't even have time to finish the second number, *Dolores de coro*.

He sank down among the wires of the pedalboard, beneath the stroboscopic lights that spun like crazed Catherine wheels, with the old Gibson still around his neck. He was blue in the face, and his heart thumped like the pedal of a bass drum. *Tum tum tutum tum*. He was immediately whisked away, and even given a tracheotomy in the ambulance so that he didn't die before he got to the hospital.

The doctor's diagnosis was merciless: 'Asphyxia from a cocktail of hard drugs.'

He remained unconscious till dawn, when the colour of his face turned from ashen to waxy pink and his pulse slowly began to pump again. They found him with his heart shattered, his brain short-circuited, his liver in rags, his testicles fit only for dog food. They treated him with Inderal, Diazepam, oxygen in the Tendelenburg position (head down), and immersed him several times in a tub of cold water to protect him against temperatures any higher than 40 degrees, such as when the sun beat down on Abacrasta. Then they let him rest for a while, before starting the second phase, known as 'initial abstinence'.

After he was discharged, his long-term therapy continued in Abacrasta. His parents had modernised the house, adding electric lights, a bathroom with gleaming tiles decorated with enamelled fish and sea horses, colour televisions, a kitchen with formica surfaces and an electric oven, fake leather sofas and armchairs, beds with soft mattresses six inches thick, a new washing machine, a fridge and a freezer for long-term planning.

They had papered his bedroom with posters of famous singers and in the middle of one wall they had put up a poster of Lazzaru himself, wearing studded leather, silver bracelets, an earring, and a gemstone in his nose. 'Lazzaru: the exploding bomb of rock!' Meanwhile he was firing bombs of a different sort into his veins, in an ever more dangerous challenge. He was playing with fire, and had known as much since he had started enjoying this kind of kick before one of his earliest concerts.

'Try a bit of this!' a sound-man had said to him. 'Forget your wine! This stuff really goes off with a bang!'

Lazzaru started going mad for the kind of explosions that went off with a smell of burning cordite and let him forget the frustrations and deprivations of the past. He lived in a state of constant intoxication, looking for bread better than the kind made of flour, as they say in Abacrasta. Over time, the game went up a few notches: acid, cocaine, heroin, concoctions of all kinds of pills washed down with alcohol.

The most difficult period in his process of recovery was the first winter without any stuff. It was a year of ice and wind, the window panes vibrated till they almost shattered with cold. Spasms snapped like dogs at his muscles, cramps wrung out his innards as if they were floor cloths. He suffered from permanent insomnia, agitation, an oppressive feeling of anxious insecurity. He trembled at the slightest sound, he jumped each time the doorbell rang.

It was during that horrible winter that the Voice called him. The sun had just risen, and he had been left alone in the house. The walls seemed to close in on him like an enormous vagina, and the gloom that brought the monsters of the night left him breathless.

'Ajò! Get ready, for your time has come!'

He saw a hand emerging lightly from the darkness and went to the drawer for one of his studded belts. He chose a black one, the longest one he had. As he climbed up to the balcony at the top of the stairs, to find the iron bar which was fixed to the wall, he found the barefoot blind woman sitting on the top step.

'What's the idea?' asked Redenta Tiria. 'Tired of living before you see forty? Aren't you ashamed of yourself? Place yourself in God's grace and learn to live with your feet on the ground, for humans are not meant to fly!'

Lazzaru Perdisciu, convinced that he was looking at a vision, did not reply. He was sure he had seen Santa Lucia in person. And that was enough for him. He went back to his room and, serene at heart, switched on the amp. He plugged in, embraced his old Gibson and launched into the solo from *Sunshine Of Your Love*.

From that moment onwards the sun of Abacrasta began to shine for him, too. Now he has opened a musical instrument shop in Noroddile and has set up a little recording studio where he discovers and launches new talent, pointing out the dangers that lie along the road to success. He married Brigitta Bruscheris, and all that she bears from those days gone by is a tattoo in the shape of a butterfly below her belly button, a mark of those nights on the stage when they thought they were flying without wings. They have four little children, who wouldn't swap running through the streets of Chentu Canes for the loveliest toys in the world. When they come and spend the weekend or the summer holidays there, they run and jump like foals, barefoot, always barefoot.

19

Concerning the author's encounter with Redenta Tiria

To conclude, it is not my purpose to convince you that the stories you have just read really happened. Should you have any doubts, at least trust what the narrator saw in the first person, saw with his own eyes, touched with his own hands. I met Redenta the blind woman on the day of my retirement.

It was so cold you could have cut the air with a scythe blade, as on that far-off Christmas Eve in 1950. There were the usual good wishes for a healthy old age, panettone with raisins, spumante tasting of cork and sorrel, and the letter of commendation from the administration signed on parchment by the mayor.

Before evening set in, in defiance of a sky filled with

clouds that heralded the coming snow storm, I got into the car to go to the big oak tree, the one from which my grandfather, Menelau Graminzone, had hanged himself. My mouth was filled with the taste of plums from Mannai Juvanna's vegetable garden, I felt the itch of her rough nails on the back of my neck, and I remembered her words:

'"Ajò! Prepare yourself, for your time has come!" That's all it says, Battì! Then it holds out an invisible hand and takes you away.'

To that voice, which I had not yet heard, I had sacrificed even my love for Cosima Thonca, a secretary who came every day from Thilipirches, so beautiful that the very sight of her would have made your legs tremble and your trousers bulge. She never missed an opportunity to come to my office for a chat, hoping to excavate, one spadeful at a time, the layers of earth beneath which I had hidden my soul. It was buried in a sea of papers and ink, in search of pleasures less ephemeral than those normally encountered in the life of a civil servant.

In the end I couldn't reach my soul. I sat down at my computer, called myself a hundred names, gave myself a thousand different faces, died and was reborn through the keyboard in the stories I had begun to write as a way of burying dead time. I had a house that I owned, a turbo-diesel car, a few savings to pay for a fine funeral, and literary ambitions that nobody gave a damn about.

I did once send a story to feature in the summer pages

of one of the island's daily newspapers, and they replied that it was too crude, hopeless. The people on the beach wanted to read something more edifying and amusing, lies to conceal their boredom.

From that moment on I wrote with even greater conviction, wanting to become famous even after my death – the sole earthly consolation of great writers. Every night I made a twelve-cup pot of coffee, and stayed at my keyboard till dawn, telling stories about what happened in Abacrasta, sure that in this way the whole world would know all about it. Yet we had a terrible reputation, and the other inhabitants concealed this fact from themselves.

During the holidays, my passport in my pocket, I had seen enough of the world to have no illusions, not to fall prey to the temptation to form a family and baptise a series of unhappy children. In Bucharest and Prague, Paris and Los Angeles and Rio de Janeiro, people laughed and suffered alike, pretending to be alive. All that changed was the landscape that framed them and the language that gave vent to the thousand discomforts of keeping up appearances.

The fire of writing that blazed within me on the first day of my retirement had gone out. *Pff!* Like that, all of a sudden, as if a horse had pissed on it. I tried to revive it with grappa, but it didn't work. I just ended up with a rotten headache and a pain in the stomach as if I'd been stabbed with a knife.

Suddenly, at about five o'clock in the afternoon, I had felt like the most wretched man in the world, an idiot who had lived only on behalf of third parties, stealing rotten grapes from the vines of others. And I cursed the day when I had begun to write, telling myself what a fool I had been not to live like everyone else, with games of cards and *morra*, christenings, confirmations, weddings, funerals, lunches with three hundred people — a nobody in the middle of nothing.

And the dead could go screw themselves; perhaps they'd understood everything and nothing in advance. For them, their brains devoured by the malignant tumour of the day-to-day, I had gambled half a century of life. For them, and for that damned pleasure that comes from writing, more insidious than any pleasure given by the saints, or wine, or women.

Cosima Thonca had laid herself out for me on a plate a thousand times, and I had always spurned her, creating an invisible chastity belt around myself. To keep from thinking of her sometimes, when I fell asleep in front of my computer screen, I would wind up an old alarm clock that rang every five minutes.

Sometimes she sneaked her way into my dreams anyway, dressed in a shawl like Santa Lucia's, mouth dirty with lipstick and eyes thick with heavy mascara. She never had time to get undressed, because the alarm clock went off first, cock-a-doodle-dooing like a tuneless cockerel.

One night she just had time to say a few words that I've never fully understood:

'Battì, you're the only man who's ever had me without having me!' God knows what she'd have said to me if she'd continued.

Mama Spredda was always worried on my behalf, she feared that the Voice would come all of a sudden, to take away the only son who still lived in her house. She must have been eighty, but she looked much less, as if God had wanted to take the time stolen from everyone else and give it all to her.

Since the death of Babbu Erricu, she had worn mourning even in the summer, black on black, from her shoes to her stockings, her pleated skirts to her blouses. Only her hair had assumed a colour of burnt stubble, smoke-grey run through with curls of a darker colour. She had four married sisters on the mainland, and a brother who had sold his animals and become a Trappist monk.

Death could come and knock at your door all of a sudden, like a thirsty beggarman, a sly thief, a ruined whore. It was better to be ready, in your black garb, hands joined, a rosary in your pocket.

I went to see my brother Martine a few times, to bring him fresh news from Abacrasta and tell him about the book I was writing. He had withdrawn into a little-known French abbey, the one at Notre-Dame-d'Acey, near Besançon.

185

The first time I went there, after a tortuous climb on foot through the hills, I felt as if I was in Abacrasta: all that was missing was the rocky landscape. The air was the same, the same sky pierced by the thin tip of a spire rising above the cross vaulting of a bell tower. In Abacrasta we had the bell tower of Santu Boddoi, which looked out over the countryside like a cross-eyed owl.

Martine speaks five languages, but he also has a good memory for Sardinian. He told me he still uses it in prayers when he wants to ask God to take special care of his island, and the earth-bound shipwrecked souls who live there.

Of that abbey I remember the four chapels surrounding the apse, the white windows, the chant of the friars, the thundering organ, the scent of lavender from the pews and walls, the light, the great light that didn't come from the sun.

Of Martine, I can still hear the sound of his sandals brushing the terracotta tiles of the central nave. *Slosh, slosh, slosh.* The sound of wet dishes, broad waves gently lapping on a beach.

My sisters I only ever hear on the telephone, asking about Mamma's health, finding out whether we've sold the rest of the land and the family home. Money's what they want, just money, because where they live it's clearly all that counts. They've never returned to Abacrasta, they're afraid that their children will catch 'the disease', and the Voice will call them.

186

I got tired of waiting for the Voice, so I went in search of it beneath the big oak of Mannoi Menelau Graminzone, on the boundary between the lands of Sas Animas and the shrine of the Madonna of the Harvest.

As I climbed higher, it began to snow. Flakes the size of pigeon feathers. In my mouth, the taste of bitter plums and brackish tears that flowed for no reason. I turned out the headlights and took my hands off the steering-wheel for a few moments, hoping to end up in some ravine. The car proceeded on its own, driven by some invisible presence. Perhaps it was the same presence that had accompanied my pointless days, holding me by the hand like a child who had never grown up.

The house, the degree, the job, football, loneliness, my mother suggesting a new engagement every day.

'You're a bird who's never learned to fly!' she told me one day, cutting me to the quick and sweeping my past away in the blink of an eye.

She meant that I had never learned to live, that the paper wings of books are as fragile as dragonflies' wings, they crumble to dust in the light of the sun.

I've lost count of the books I've read in my life, but I can't remember a single beginning or ending by heart. I see everything in fragments, as though in a giant kaleidoscope in which the distorted faces of the living and the dead of Abacrasta collide and mingle, merging into a single book, perhaps the one I'm writing.

I didn't do military service, either, because of a general friend of my father's who had told me my chest was too weak to fight. I had seen the sea only from the deck of a ship, a huge basin of molten lead ploughed by spittle-flecked billows.

By the time I got out of the car the snow was up to my ankles, it crunched beneath my shoes like powdered cork. I had to cover the last part of the journey on foot, as my grandfather had done that night. I looked at my watch: it was exactly seven o'clock.

All of a sudden it stopped snowing and the sky glowed with that great light that I had seen in the Abbey of Notre-Dame-d'Acey. The full moon appeared, bright and translucent as a sheet of caramel. The tongues of the brambles coiled with the weight of the snow. The holly berries looked like drops of blood hanging from the trees. A whirl of wind stirred the snow and pushed it up to dance a carnival dance.

Like a great wingless bird, Mannoi Graminzone appeared in the sky and began flying around.

'*Zoooommm, zooom, zooomm, ratatatata, tatata, tata* . . . Into the trench, Battì! Into the trench, the shrapnel's raining down!'

I started running and tried to get on tiptoes to get away from it, shouting:

'Take me away, *mannò*! Take me with you!'

'*Tatata, tata, ratatata* . . .'

My grandfather, even if he always signed his name with an X, had learned to fly, but he didn't know how to land. When he came back from the war, he had a coat-of-arms carved above the door, showing an aeroplane taking off. He was a restless soul, like me.

'*Zooomm, zooom, zooom* . . . *tatata, tata* . . . Go back to Abacrasta, Battì . . . *zoooom, zooo* . . . burn your books . . . *tatatata, tata* . . . buy yourself a hundred sheep and marry Cosima Thonca . . . *zoom, zooooomm* . . .'

A few minutes later, when it started snowing again, my grandfather had disappeared. I was still running towards the big oak. Beneath the trunk, in the middle of a circle of stones, sat Redenta Tiria, her face between her knees and her hands in her raven hair. She was barefoot and half-naked, wearing only a sheet of white silk that looked as if it was woven from threads of snow. She got to her feet and, crooking her finger, beckoned me to approach. A strip of her tunic was stained with blood, and her face was furrowed with deep scratches.

'Come into the circle! Don't be afraid!'

Breathlessly, I obeyed. The blind woman came over and stroked the back of my neck, as only Mannai Juvanna had done when I was a child.

'So, aren't you fed up with living without ever really having lived? You people of Abacrasta, don't you ever tire of playing *morra* with death? Haven't you worked out that death always wins, that it has a thousand

189

fingers, a thousand eyes and a thousand voices?'

'It's just . . .' She didn't even give me time to reply.

'It's just nothing! It's just that you've got to quit this habit of giving back the gift of life on the merest whim! Do you think God makes and destroys just as he sees fit? You're no longer living in the days of Eracliu Palitta and Artemisa Crapiolu. Open your eyes and see the world for what it is! There's bad blood flowing in your veins and you've spilt enough of it already, now that's enough! Go back to the village and do what your grandfather told you to do! Remember that life must end when the Great Father says so, but it can only really start when we want it to!'

'But . . .'

'But nothing! Finish that book of yours! Because you must make the dead speak, bring them back to life in stories. And you must make the living understand that the business of living may be hard to learn, but it isn't impossible. And if you are given time and money, use them to build a little sanctuary in this accursed place where your grandfather sacrificed himself. Lay at least the first stone, and call it the Sanctuary of Salvation, so that people will bring their rosaries to pray here, rather than belts or rope to hang themselves with! Write in your book that everyone can be saved, because Redenta Tiria came down to earth to cut out the Voice's tongue, to banish the soul-stealers. Now jump back and leave the circle, but without moving the stones, because otherwise the misfortunes will continue!'

As she said this a winged white horse emerged from the blanket of snow. The blind woman stroked its mane and smiled. I barely had time to ask her where she was going.

'I'm going where the beasts of prey will invite me to dinner!' she replied.

Then she climbed up on the horse and galloped away into the air, vanishing among the wisps of snow.

Glossary